SAMUEL'S PRIDE SERIES   BOOK 3

KATHI S. BARTON

WCP

World Castle Publishing, LLC
Pensacola, Florida

Copyright © Kathi S. Barton 2014
Print ISBN: 9781629891002
eBook ISBN: 9781629891019
First Edition World Castle Publishing, LLC, May 23, 2014
http://www.worldcastlepublishing.com

Licensing Notes

Cover: Karen Fuller
Editor: Eric Johnston
Editor: Maxine Bringenberg

Chapter 1

Tania Thornton—Thor as everyone called her—stood as still as she could. This was the worst part of her job, the waiting. But when movement near her on the left got her attention, she knew in a second that she'd been made. Lifting her gun, she fired twice in the direction the man had gone and took off after him. It was show time, and she wasn't in the mood to get caught this late in the game. She took him down just as he was reaching for his walkie-talkie.

Snapping his neck, she disarmed him in seconds, putting his guns and ammo in pockets all over her pants. She smiled when she thought of the nice little collection she'd amassed only in the past hour. These people were out for blood. Her mike in her ear sounded just as she noticed another guard walking the perimeter and moved to intercept him. It was time to call in the big boys on this.

"I thought I mentioned to you, oh about fifty times, that if you needed anything to call the shop. I'm in a very important meeting." Thor grinned. Her boss, Lyod Sweeney, was sounding more and more pissed every time she spoke to him. "Who the fuck is this anyway?"

"Thor." She heard him cursing and had to work hard at not laughing out loud. The guard was only about ten feet from her. "I found where Lipscomb is hiding out."

There was more cursing, and she was slightly confused by it. They'd been hunting for Ansell Lipscomb for nearly six months. When he came back on the line, she had to stop in her forward motion to kill the guard when he started yelling at her. Did he really want her to back the fuck off?

"Where the fuck are you right now? I've told you several times that he was out of the country, and now you're telling me that you're hunting for him? Do you ever listen to a word that I tell you?" She started to tell him that Ansell was on the property right now when he continued. "I want you to sit on this and wait to talk to me in the morning. Better yet, forget everything you think you know. He's not fucking here."

"But what if I told you that I've seen him at the address?" He didn't answer her, and she continued. This wasn't what she'd expected from him, not at all. "There are more guards on this property than I've seen on detail at the White House. This guy is here."

"You're here...you're at the property now?" She told him she was. "Mother fuck. Do you have any idea what you've stepped into? Get back now before you get yourself killed."

Something was off about this whole thing. But before she could ask him what the hell he was going on about, the guard she'd been running down turned suddenly as his walkie squawked at him. When he turned in her direction, Thor dropped to the ground and waited. As he walked by her, she grabbed his leg and tossed him to the ground, slicing open his throat as he fell.

"Are you fucking listening to me?" She didn't answer. The guard had had a knife she'd not seen, and she had to pull it from her ribs before she could speak. The pain radiated through her entire body, and she had to take several deep breaths before she could speak.

"I'm hurt." He said something to the effect that she was going to be hurt more when he found her, but she saw three men coming toward her. Lifting her gun up, she took out all three before she stood up. "Something must be going on. They're coming out to the grounds heavily."

"You think?" Sweeney took several long breaths, all of which echoed through her headset as she waited for him to explain. "There's no hope for it now. You're as dead as they come."

The blow to the back of her head made her pitch forward. The body that she fell on was armed, and she pulled his gun from his hand just as she fell. Turning as she landed, she lifted the gun and fired three times into the man's head just as he was lifting his gun. When he fell on top of her, she rolled quickly and found it was too late for her to shoot the next two men. She was toast. She wasn't going down without a fight, but bleeding and hurt wasn't giving her the edge that she needed. They had her before she could do much more than hurt one of them.

"You know, there is no reason for you to be this rough with me. First of all, I'm not in a position to play as rough with you as I'd like, and there are five of you to my one." The man that held her left arm grunted at her. Thor grinned and winked at him. "I think I broke your jaw. Does it hurt much?"

He jerked her arm behind her, and she felt it tear. Thor supposed she should really keep her mouth shut, but they were going to kill her anyway, so she'd have her fun. And beating the shit out of them had been a great deal of fun. They took her to a van and threw her in the back, where she blacked out for a time. When she woke, they were dragging her to a large cinderblock building.

"You're going to pay for this." The guy at her right holding her other arm cuffed her in the head. Though she saw stars, she didn't let him know she was affected by it. But the second time he hit her, she felt her teeth cut deeply into her lip.

"You do know that others know I'm here. I mean, any moment now the entire police department is going to pull in here and you're going to be sorry." He laughed, and she frowned. "You think you know something I don't?"

"I'm sure I do. And no one is coming to help you. We have it on good authority that you're alone and will always be that way. We have an inside man, so to speak." He jerked her forward and tied her to the wall that had grommets on it. She didn't bother now trying to get away. The gun pointed at her head kept her from being stupid. By the time she was secured against the wall with her legs and arms tied tightly, she knew as surely as she was standing there she was dead meat. When the men backed away, she had a second to think they were going to kill her now. But someone else had entered the little cell she'd been put in.

"Hello, Tania. I've heard a great deal about you." Thor looked at the man she'd been chasing for months. He looked impeccable in his three-piece suit and dark tie. There was not a hair out of place, and he looked like he was finding a great deal of humor in her situation.

"I've heard some shit about you, too. In fact, I have a thick file of all kinds of stuff about you. Like you're a drug runner, murderer, as well as a hired gun. Whatever will you do when you're behind bars?" He laughed at her, and she laughed as well, even though laughing was the furthest thing from her mind. "The police know you're here. I've called in backup."

"No, you have not. And as for you getting anyone to care that you're gone, that's not going to happen either. You don't even have a cat or dog to mourn your passing." The guy to her left walked up to her and rammed a knife into her shoulder. He stepped back, leaving the blade where he'd put it. "That's for killing some of my best men. You should know that each of these men in here are going to play with you, though I doubt very much any of it will be fun for you."

The next man rammed a knife into her other shoulder, and she cried out despite her trying not to scream. The pain was making her dizzy, yet she stared at Lipscomb as he sat in a chair.

"You're not going to enjoy this, I think. The men have been waiting for a while to have a little bit of fun." The bullet to her thigh startled her. When she screamed this time, she felt tears roll down her cheeks. Lipscomb found humor in that as well and laughed for five minutes. Thor simply tried to breathe through the pain.

This went on for over an hour. She knew that was all it was because Lipscomb told her so. By the time he and the men who'd abused her left her to hang there, Thor knew that it wasn't a matter of if she was going to die, but how soon. Moving her head, she pulled the first blade from her shoulder with her teeth and spit it to the floor. Blood poured from the wound, and she watched it for a few seconds. Then she closed her eyes against the pain and tried to think of something pleasant. There was nothing in her mind that would make her smile.

When she opened her eyes, she realized that she was fading fast. Looking around the room, she saw a rug on the floor and thought of a man she'd not thought of in fifteen years. Samuel Payne. And as she reached for him, just wanting someone to know that she had died, she remembered their times together. They had been each other's back.

"Did he hit you again?" He'd told her that he had. His father hit him like her dad did her. *"I hate them. Both of them. Someday I'm going to be bigger than him and I'm going to make him pay."*

Samuel had taken her hand and held it tightly in his. He had always been her best friend, and even more so when they were hiding from their abusive fathers. Thor could admit now that she'd been in love with him since the first time she'd seen him. She was drifting in and out just as she touched his mind.

~~~

Samuel tried to shy away from the pain. He had no idea what had happened to him, but he hurt in more places than he thought he had places to hurt. But something was off, and when someone touched his mind, he knew that it wasn't him but whoever it was that disturbed his sleep. Then the memories came of when the two of them were just children.

"You'll not be able to kill him. It's not allowed." The girl, Thor, had snorted at him. "And you should know that it's my job to protect you, not you getting yourself all hurt trying to kill him. Someday I'll be much bigger than them and I'll take them out."

"Don't be an idiot. You know that I can do just as much as you can. Didn't I just prove to you that I could pee standing up?" He laughed with her. "Course I got it all over my shoes, but I still did it."

"So you did." Samuel remembered now with a full clarity that he and Thor, as she'd wanted everyone to call her, had been hiding in the basement of an abandoned house. He'd been beaten by his dad just that day, and she'd taken one from her dad the day before. Neither of them were in any shape to defend themselves from anyone. The nudge at his mind had him concentrating on it rather than the painful memories that had apparently come from her.

"I'm dying." Samuel sat up in bed and looked around the room. It sounded as if she were right there with him.

"Thor?" Her laughter made him get up. She was in pain, and he could feel it like his own. "Where are you? I want to come to you."

"Too late for that, I'm afraid." He looked at Kennedy when she sat up in bed. Her belly was swollen with their first child, but all he could think about at that moment was his friend. *"I'm dying, and there ain't shit you can do to save me. Not this time. They stabbed me and shot me up pretty good. Not what I thought would happen to me. I was trying to get the bad guys."*

"Tell me where you are." He got a pencil and paper and wrote down for Kennedy to contact Jimmy and get him there. She nodded and lifted her phone to call him. "I'm getting dressed now. I'm coming to you, and you'd better not be dead."

"My God, you're still trying to save me, aren't you? I'm in Ohio. Far away from you. You just need to come and get my body. I don't want to hang here to rot." He started to tell her that he was in the same state when she continued. *"I don't think I can remember the address, but the house is owned by an*

Ansell Combs. He's a drug king, and his real name is Lipscomb. Not very bright in the change of his name if you ask me."

Jimmy came into the room just as he pulled on his jacket. Samuel was glad to see that he'd dressed for a run, dark clothes as well as a gun strapped to his hip. Right behind him was Gab, and she, too, was ready.

"I need an address now." They headed to the office as he explained what he knew. Samuel tried several times to contact Thor again, but she had either passed out or she was being hurt again. Her pain beat at him. Neither option was something he wanted to think about. They were able to pull an address by the time she spoke again.

"Do you remember that time when we were going to run away?" He remembered and told her so. *"I wish your mom hadn't talked us out of it. We might have gotten killed, but we would have been together. I'm all alone in this world. Are you?"*

"No. I have a wife with a baby on the way." He felt her weakening and told her to buck up. "If you're dead when I get there, I'm going to pound your ass."

"I'm so sorry about this. I don't know why I bothered you, but I was afraid of dying alone. I never got me that cat I was telling you about. The one that had one green and one blue eye. Do you remember her?"

She was babbling, and he knew it. Trying to keep her talking was draining him, and he wasn't sure what to say to her when she started talking about things that she'd done in her life. Things he was sure that she'd never shared with another living soul. Then she bounced back to when they were kids.

"Thor, we're coming. I should be there in an hour. I want you to hang on for me." She told him she'd try. "Good girl. I want you to meet my wife and my friends. Mother will be so pissed at you if you don't come and see her garden."

"Garden? Your mom has a garden? What does your dad think of that? He probably chops the heads off the plants before she can pick them." She started singing to him, and he had to smile. She couldn't carry a tune back then and certainly couldn't now.

When contact with her stopped, he knew that she still lived but not for long. Samuel could feel her body weakening and was terrified that they'd be too late. He looked over at Jimmy when he cleared his throat.

"What is she?" It took Samuel a few seconds to think what he'd been asking. And when he started to answer, Jimmy continued. "The reason I ask is because I've known you for nearly all your life, and I've never seen you get this worked up over a girl before Kennedy."

"We were children together. And she's a human last I saw her. She could...we could communicate with each other, but we never figured out why, nor did we tell anyone. She was just...she was my savior as a child. Probably more than my mom had been. Then one day she simply disappeared. I haven't thought of her in years."

"But she knew to contact you when she was in trouble." Samuel didn't know why she'd done it now either, and hoped that he got to ask her. "I don't like this. Do you know why she's where she is?"

"Nope. But she said she was dying and wanted me to come and get her body. She said she didn't want to rot where she was." Samuel thought about what else she'd said. "I think she's being tortured. She said they had stabbed and shot her up."

The address they were at was surrounded by a tall fence, the kind that said don't even try it or you're dead. Jimmy parked the car, and they both got out and started to undress. They'd be better at getting in as their beasts than humans anyway. By the time they were moving along the property, Kaleb and Stephen had joined them. Each of them paired up and took off around the entire place looking for a way in. After about twenty minutes, Stephen came to find him.

"I've taken Jimmy in, and he's hunting for any sign of her. We've managed to deplete the number of guards, too. Nine so far that we've seen. What is this girl? Anyway, I got tired of walking around." Stephen grinned. "I'll take you and Kaleb in if you promise not to scratch me up."

"Can't make any promises. Besides," Kaleb started, "a man like you should know better than to wear a fancy suit to a hunting party. You might mess up that silk shirt of yours."

Samuel wanted them to simply shut up, but he knew that tensions were running high and let Stephen take him first. Shifting quickly then dressing, he was running toward the smell of blood when Jimmy told him he'd found the building.

None of them would look at him when he got there. Samuel knew then that they were too late. When Jimmy walked toward him, he started shaking his head. He didn't want to hear that she was dead.

"She's in there, but…you should be prepared for what you see. I've only gotten a small glimpse of her because of the guards they have just inside the building, but if she makes it back with us it'll be a miracle. She's…Christ, Samuel, they did things to her that I don't think I've ever seen done to anyone, much less a human." Jimmy looked back at the building before continuing. "She's hung from chains, and it will take some work to get her down. Then we'll need for her to be taken to the hospital to —"

"The clinic." Jimmy looked over his shoulder, then back at him before he nodded. He knew who was behind him, knew since he'd gotten there that Stephen had been assigned to hold him back in the event that something went wrong. "I'll let them know she's coming and that at all costs they're to save her."

"I can't change her." Samuel turned to look at Stephen when he spoke. "I don't know what she is, but she's not wholly human, not if she can talk to you like she has. I'll give her blood to help her along, but I can't...I don't know what kind of person she is."

Samuel understood. When a vampire or any other supe changed a person to one of them, they were responsible for them. Forever. And if they fucked up, became a rogue or killed anyone even if by accident, the one who changed them was responsible for it as much as they were. Nodding once, Samuel braced himself to enter the room. Kaleb was given the signal, and he tore the door from the wall.

"Mother fuck." Samuel had no idea who had said it, but he felt it was an understatement. But before he could go to her, three guards, all of them human, rushed them. In seconds they were dead, and they made their way to his friend.

"What did she do to piss them off this badly?" Vinnie moved closer to her as he continued to whisper. "They didn't want her to die quickly, that's for sure. There are nine...no ten knives in her."

But the knives weren't all they'd used on her. There were seven bullet holes in her legs alone, and her arms had been sliced in long ribbons of open flesh. Her face, what he could see of it, looked as if it had been used as a punching bag. Moving toward her, Samuel said her name.

When she lifted her head slightly and then let it drop again, he felt the bile in his belly rise to his throat. He'd been wrong. She'd not been used as a punching bag, but someone had flayed her open and left the skin hanging where it had been cut, making her look like raw meat.

"Samuel." He realized that Kaleb had said his name several times when the man hit him. "I need you to back away from her so we can cut her down. She's going to scream if I don't miss my bet, and that might bring more shit down on us."

He couldn't touch her, but while he watched, he contacted the clinic with his cell phone to let them know that Stephen was coming in with an emergency. When he was finished, Samuel wanted to pull her into his arms and hold her, tell her it would be all right, but he wasn't sure. There was no way she'd make it to the next breath, much less to the clinic. When the chains were broken from her wrists by Vinnie, she did scream, but not loud enough to bring anyone running. It had been more of a whimper, and that hurt him more.

Kaleb backed away from her, but Samuel noticed that he held her hand. He wished that he could hold her as well, but knew that he'd break down if he did. Letting Stephen near her, he watched as the large vampire opened his vein at his wrist and pressed it to her mouth. When his blood spilled from her mouth to trail down her already bloodied cheek, Kaleb leaned to her ear and whispered something to her. After a few more tension-filled seconds, she swallowed.

Before long, she was breathing better and her heart started to beat just a little quicker. Stephen picked her up and stared long at Kaleb before he turned to Samuel with hopefulness in his eyes that surprised him.

"I'll take her now. Have you let them know how bad she is?" Samuel nodded. "Then I'll meet you back at the clinic. I won't leave her until you get there. But I wouldn't dally if I were you."

They made their way across the compound. None of them spoke, but they did work together every time they came upon a set of guards. By the time they got to where they'd entered, they noticed that Kaleb was no longer with them. Just as he was going to go and find the big bear, he came toward them.

"Where did you run off to? Didn't you hear that we had to get to the clinic?" Kaleb nodded but said nothing. "I was ready to leave your ass behind."

"I needed to do something." When he didn't explain, Samuel turned from him. Whatever it had been, it wasn't going to get them to the clinic any sooner, so he let it go.

Chapter 2

"What do you mean there's no one there? I left two dozen men. Are you telling me that they all left their post?" Ansell shook his head and sat down at his long dining room table. Lyod hated when he gave him that smile. It was like he was saying that Lyod was so stupid that he didn't want to startle him into being violent. "What are you saying then?"

"They're dead. All of them. As for the girl, she's gone too, but not dead, just...gone." Lyod sat down hard. "When I had one of my men go over to finish her off, he called me to tell me that he'd found all their bodies. Some of them looked as if a wild animal had torn at them. The rest?" His shrug was not encouraging.

"The rest were what?" Fear settled over him gently. He'd been afraid all of his career that he'd be caught at helping Ansell and thought that this was it. The Feds had come in and found his little side job.

"Mutilated. Most of them had their throats ripped out. Two of them...well, let's just say that identification of them will be next to impossible. And those were the sixteen we found. The rest were in pieces all over the compound."

Lyod frowned. Ansell was lying to him. He had no idea why, but there was no way that his men were killed at close combat.

"What happened to Thornton?"

Ansell shrugged as he poured himself a cup of tea. The man had a prissiness about him that drove Lyod nuts. But he paid him well. And for that alone he could put up with him.

"I'm having the video looked at again by an expert. From what I've heard and seen, there is nothing there. I was told that the feed wasn't shut off so much as it's just blank." Picking up his cup with his pinkie finger sticking out like a dick, he sipped at his drink before continuing. "The time stamp is there so it's running, but there is nothing to indicate what happened. It looks like all the cameras were blacked out. But they were not."

Lyod tried to think what might have happened, and where Thornton was. She was not just a small liability but a major one. She could take them down with one word, and he knew it. Before he could say anything else, his cell phone went off...the private one, not his business. Answering it, he waited for the person on the other end to speak first. He nearly fell off his chair when he did.

"Turn on the news. Apparently someone notified them about the shit that went down at the cells." Lyod asked if there was a television nearby and was told in the den. As both he and Ansell went to view it, Tyler continued. "They are saying it was an animal attack. But they seem to be holding back that there were guns there as well as blood all over the yard. They're saying sixteen dead so far. What the fuck happened? Who called them?"

"I did," Ansell answered when Lyod asked him. "I thought it best that we put this out there before whoever took her tells. This way we can control the situation and if it leaks without us, then they may say whatever they wish. The animal attack is my idea."

Lyod doubted that anything would be contained from this if the pictures from the aerial view were any indication. There were sheets all over the place, it seemed. He was glad now that he'd been able to keep his name off the property lease. He didn't need this shit coming back to bite him in the ass.

After assuring Tyler, his right-hand man, that things were going to be all right, he asked him to watch the hospitals and morgues. Tyler told him he'd already started on that when he'd heard that Thor was gone. Lyod sat down across from Ansell to talk. They had to figure out what happened to Thornton, and the sooner the better. Right now only Ansell was involved, but he'd throw Lyod under the bus so fast that he'd never see it coming. Lyod knew that he needed to make this right, and as soon as possible.

"I thought you assured me that no one would come for her." Lyod didn't get the chance to tell him that no one would when he continued. "She's not going to be able to identify you, but me she will. I'm not at all happy with you at the moment."

"I don't blame you. Neither am I. When we left her, she was as good as dead. They took their time with her, cutting her up so badly it's doubtful her own mother would know who she was." Ansell nodded. "And if she is alive or was when she left the cell, she'd be hard pressed to live longer than it would take for them to get her to any hospital."

"When you find her, living or dead, I want to know. I owe the girl. She killed five of my best men before we were able to get her under control." Ansell leaned back in his chair and stared at him. This was it, Lyod thought, he's going to try and kill me. Sliding his hand into his pocket where his gun was, he put his finger on the trigger and waited. Ansell cleared his throat before he spoke again. "What do you know about the shipment that is coming in on Thursday?"

It took him several seconds to catch up. "Shipment? You mean the drugs? I've made arrangements to have the entire load picked up as soon as it's brought in. There should be about seventy tons of it already cut and the sixty thousand pounds you wanted cut again. I have my teams already set up to divvy it up to our street teams."

The long pause had him nervous, but he didn't shift on his seat like he wanted to. When Ansell handed him a file, he took it but didn't open it until Ansell started talking. The pictures on the first page made him look up.

"Do you know that man?" Lyod told him he didn't. "He's the man responsible for my last two shipments coming in short. He works for me. I'd like for you to take care of his family for me."

"Do you have an address?" Ansell handed him another sheet of paper. "I'll have someone get on to this right—"

"No. I'd prefer you did it. Call it a payment for fucking this up with Thornton. You owe me this much and maybe just a tad more." Ansell sat back in his chair and smiled. "You wish to argue with me?"

"No. I'll get it done." He had no problem killing for the man. He'd made Lyod as wealthy as he'd wanted to be, and there was more to come. "I'll have it done by the weekend. You want the man dead as well?"

"Oh no. That won't be necessary. I would like for him to continue working for me, and this will give him an incentive to do better. And bring me pictures. I'd like to show them to him whenever he gets it in his head to steal from me again." Lyod nodded and put the file back on his desk. There was no way he'd be able to leave with it anyway. Looking at the address again, Lyod committed it to his memory. Ansell was shredding that even before he continued with what he wanted done.

"The child can be done quickly if you'd like. But the wife, I want her to suffer in ways that would make what my men did to Thornton look like a walk in the park. She will be your greatest gift to me." Lyod nodded. He'd get to play. That's all he really cared about. "As for the staff, kill them as well. Leave them all where he sees them first thing."

Lyod decided that he'd leave for the house first thing in the morning and spend the day playing. He felt his dick get hard at just the thought of what he was going to do to any of the females in the house. A few minutes later, he left the mansion and headed to the office. Things were about to get nasty for the young detective as well.

Thornton had started off on the wrong foot so far as Lyod was concerned. Her first day on the squad had him wanting to transfer her out of his little house and onto someone else. But she'd made a name for herself with the higher-ups and there was no budging them. The mayor had told him point blank that if he didn't like her, she'd stay and Lyod would be gone. He'd been playing nice with her since that day three years ago.

"Hey, boss. Did you see the papers?" Lyod told Simon Dickless that he'd seen the news, too. Dickless wasn't really his name, but Lyod had never been one to remember anyone when he couldn't benefit from them. "What do you suppose went down that would have all them armed guys running around? The zoo is saying that they've accounted for all their wild animals, too."

Lyod wished he had someone at the zoo. It would have been easy to have one of the big cats killed off and laid out there to take the blame. Now someone was going to have him searching for this thing when all he wanted to do was find Thornton. When Dickless said something about Thornton, he asked him to repeat it.

"She's not in. I'm thinking she might still be on that stakeout she'd been talking about yesterday. I think she might have a handle on one of the big ten." The big ten was what their department called the top ten on the FBI's most wanted. There were so many names on the list that no one believed that any of them would ever be found. But Thornton had managed to find two already. Fucking cunt.

"I don't suppose you know where it was, do you?" Dickless shook his head. "Then I suggest that you shut the fuck up and get back to work. When you have something solid on her, tell me. Otherwise, keep your speculations to yourself."

He was opening the door to his office when Dickless told him the mayor was in there. Lyod decided that the next time he needed a fall guy, Dickless was going to go down. The mother fucker knew how much he hated the mayor. Hell, even the mayor did. But there was no going back now. He knew he was there.

"What can you tell me about the compound that had two dozen armed men on it?" Not even a "hi, how the hell are you?" "I want answers as of ten minutes ago. And so you know, I hate finding out this shit from the papers.

Damn near had to run over a news reporter when they were camped out on my lawn wanting answers."

"I know as much as you do. There were sixteen armed men found on the property in various stages of being torn apart. There wasn't any other animals there other than the smallish kind that were feeding on them. The call came in around five-thirty from someone who didn't leave a name." Lyod sat at his desk and found a file opened to the information that he'd requested from his assistant on his way in, but most of this shit he knew. "The property belongs to someone by the name of Dan Enterprises. They manufactured pallets. But the company went belly-up about five years ago. So far as I know it's not been sold since then."

At least that's what they'd find if they went to find anything about it in the records downtown. That little bit of work had cost him dearly, too. He looked up when Mayor Reese Horne started cursing.

"Where is Thor? I want her on this case." Lyod took great pleasure it telling him that she'd not come in today. "Did you send someone out to her place to see what's wrong with her?"

"Why would I do that?" Horne looked at him as if he couldn't believe him. "I mean, I don't know what's she's doing. For all I know, she's shacked up with some shit hole and is having sex for the first time in her life."

He knew he'd gone too far the moment the man sitting in front of him stood up. There was anger boiling off him, and Lyod would have been a fool to say anything else. Instead he waited.

"Do you have any idea what this woman has done for this department? Just last month she managed to single-handedly thwart a robbery and made sure that several thousand people were not killed when she discovered that there was a madman in the airport with a bomb. What the fuck have you done?" Before he could tell the man that he'd been there with her, Horne continued. "As of right now, it is your duty—no, your number one priority—to find her and make sure she's not injured. I want reports from you hourly until you have solid information. Do I make myself perfectly clear?"

"Yes, sir." As soon as Horne left the office, Lyod sat down. "Fucking cunt. She'll have my job when she gets back. *If* she gets back."

Lyod did what the mayor demanded of him, and put it out there that Thornton was missing and sent a car to her home. That took nothing more than sending one of the men out. Apparently they all knew where she lived but him. He fucking hated the woman.

~~~

Samuel was surprised to find Kaleb in the room with Thor, more so to find him sleeping in the chair next to the bed. When he sat up, Samuel asked him how long he'd been there.

"About midnight. She's not moved. The nurses said that her blood pressure is rising and her temp has come up a few degrees as well." Kaleb stood and stretched before continuing. "Did you know that she's a cop?"

"No. I haven't heard from her in years. When we were kids together, she and I used to…I guess protect each other. Fat lot of good it did either of us, but we did have each other when it didn't seem we had anyone else." Samuel sat down in the chair that Kaleb vacated. As Kaleb walked to the window, Samuel thought about Kaleb leaving them at the scene. "What did you have to do that was so important the other night when we were leaving with her?"

He didn't think he was going to answer him. Kaleb continued to look out the window and not at him. There had always been something so different about his friend. Other than being a grizzly, Samuel realized that he knew very little about his friend and wondered if anyone really did. Kaleb Jonas had always been very quiet and reserved.

"I had to get a few more scents." Kaleb turned then and leaned against the wall. "She's my mate. I'm not really sure what to do about it, but I wanted you to know. And another thing you should be aware of — I've given her my blood. It has...."

When he didn't finish, Samuel felt his lion shift under his skin. Not really fear dusted along his skin, but something close to it. For whatever reason Kaleb had not to finish right then, Samuel was sure he didn't want to know. The nurse walking in had them both shifting away from the bed and out into the hall. They had to fix her bandages.

"There you are." He smiled at his wife as she moved down the hall toward them. "I thought I'd find you here. Did you know that there is a guard at every entrance of this place, and they're practically giving everyone the shake down before they can come in?" Kennedy looked at him, but he didn't have a clue what was going on. Before he could ask her more about it, Kaleb spoke up.

"That would be because of me. I put them in place when I realized that she might be in danger. Or us if they come here to find her. Whoever had her wanted her dead. I'm not willing to let that happen." When Kaleb didn't tell Kennedy that Thor was his mate, he didn't either.

Samuel wanted answers but wasn't sure really what to ask to get them. When they were let back into the room, some of the bandages on Thor's face had been removed. She'd healed a great deal in the four days she'd been there. He glanced at Kaleb but said nothing.

"I've been to the doctor. She said that I'm doing fine and that I will need to take it easy for the next few days." Kennedy grinned. "We have nine days left and we'll be parents. I'm so excited and terrified at the same time."

Samuel wasn't afraid to admit he was terrified as well. Excited yes, but scared shitless about having something so small depending on him. He could barely walk into a room without making something fall to the floor and shatter. What the hell was he supposed to do with a baby? A movement on the bed had them all standing and tensing up.

"She's not moved before," Kaleb whispered to the room as he moved a lock of Thor's hair from her forehead. "I'm not ready for her to wake yet."

"Why not?" Kaleb looked at Kennedy when she asked just as quietly. "I, for one, would like to know who did this to her and kick their ass. No one treats anyone this way and gets away with it."

"I'll take care of them." Kaleb said it with so much finality that Samuel almost felt sorry for whoever did this to Thor. "I have some of their scents now, and they'll not get away."

Kennedy looked at Samuel, then back at Kaleb. He knew that she got it, and when she smiled he did as well. There would be no stopping her from throwing these two together if either of them had any plans of not going through with their mating business. Samuel knew that Kaleb was a good man, but the man had never said anything about what he'd do with a mate. Kaleb had said he didn't want or need one, but having one staring right at you like this was something different altogether. He wondered how hard Thor would fall before she finally let him into her life, because Samuel had no doubt that she'd be the hardest one to convince.

A sudden movement on the bed had his lion run to the front. Thor had grabbed Kaleb's wrist and held it. Her eyes were swollen almost shut, but she'd turned to him. Neither of them moved.

"I won't hurt you." Kaleb put his hand on hers. "I swear to you I won't hurt you. Let me go, love, and rest."

Compulsion was there, even Samuel could feel it, but she didn't let Kaleb go. When he peeled her fingers from his skin, Samuel noticed that she'd bled on his arm. When he settled her hand back on her chest, Kaleb licked the blood off. Samuel wondered if the man knew that he'd just exchanged blood with his mate to begin the process of claiming her.

"I know what I did." Samuel looked at his friend when he whispered in his mind. *"I need to speak to you. There are things that I need to tell you. Something I should have told you years ago."*

"Are you more than a shifter?" Kaleb nodded but didn't speak. *"Am I going to hate this?"*

"More than likely." Samuel nodded and sat back down. Kaleb said he was going home to take a shower and would be back soon. He left after taking Thor's hand in his and kissing it. This was not the kick-ass Kaleb he knew.

He had no idea how a bear claimed his mate or, for that matter, if that's how it worked at all. Being a leader of all sorts of animals was the hardest thing Samuel had ever done. How the hell was he supposed to keep up with the way they did things, much less keep them all happy? Samuel looked up when Kennedy sat on his lap.

"I love you." He nuzzled her neck when she spoke. "The girl there, what does she mean to you? More than a friend, I think. Do I need to *choilleadh* you? Or hurt her?"

Samuel knew the word. She was asking him if she needed to castrate him. He nipped at her neck and held her tighter, laying his hand over her belly to feel their child move beneath it.

"When I was seven and she five, we found each other one night after my father had beaten me so badly that I could barely move. I'd found this place about a month before and would go there to hide from him until my mom came home from work. Apparently Thor used it as well when her own dad had taken a belt to her." Kennedy put her hand over his and moved it over her belly to where the baby was moving. He continued telling her what this girl meant to him as his own child flipped and moved against his hand. "She'd been beaten as well that night. Her back was bloodied, and her face.... It wasn't as bad as she'd been when we brought her in, but he'd taken his fist to her. I wondered how she could even see."

"Her mother, where was she when her little girl was being abused?" Samuel remembered that she'd been alive and wondered if Mrs. Thornton was as yet, but he told Kennedy that he didn't know. Thor had never mentioned her when they'd been children.

"One night, when I'd decided that my dad wasn't going to hit my mom again, Thor talked me out of it. While she said I could take him—I was about nine by then—I could never look my mom in the face if I'd been responsible for killing him. Instead, she and I devised a plan to make him suffer. If I remember correctly, it was the best two weeks I had while he spent that time in the hospital." Kennedy laughed and asked him what she'd done. "She iced up our front steps and made him fall down them. Broke three ribs and his left leg. Thor had never been one to back down when she felt someone had 'shit in her oatmeal,' as she used to say."

"Oh, I like her. Very much so. Do you think she could teach me a thing or two about dealing with bullies?"

Christ, he hoped not. His wife was pretty fierce now. And since she'd been at the end of her pregnancy, she'd been a tad on the violent side. Instead of answering her, he kissed her. Samuel didn't think it would distract her for very long, but it might buy him a little time to tell her that she was just fine the way she was, thanks.

Chapter 3

The room wasn't overly bright. Thor knew it wasn't, but it was still painful to look around. There was a fuzzy blob in front of her, but other than it being large, she had no idea what or even who it might be. She closed her eyes and opened them again when she heard the laughter.

"You're not going to be able to lay there pretending you're asleep this time. I've let it go before, but not this time." She tried to bring the man into focus, but it was simply too hard.

"I don't know you." Laughter again. "I think you are very rude to laugh at me when I've been beat to shit and — Fuck. Where am I?" She had to close her eyes again. The pain was overwhelming and making her slightly sick to her stomach.

"You're at the hospital, one that will protect you at all costs." She snorted. There was no way anyone could protect her from Lipscomb. He was a motherfucker with a god-like attitude. "Don't you believe me? I've never lied to you before."

This time he was closer to her. The brown eyes looked familiar, but she couldn't think beyond hurting. Reaching out to touch him caused her more pain, but she had to see who he was. As soon as he was close enough, she realized who he was.

"Samuel." He nodded and kissed the palm of her hand. "I've missed you so much. You came for me."

"I did. You did tell me to, didn't you? And when I got there, you didn't even have cake or any beer." She moved back on the bed and laid there for several seconds, trying to think how to tell him that he needed to stay away from her. "Oh honey, who did this to you? Thor? Who did this to you?"

"I work for some pretty powerful people. And I'm not sure, but I think maybe I've stepped in more than I can get out of." She turned to look at him. "It would be better if I don't tell you anything right now."

While Samuel nodded, she knew that he wasn't satisfied. That was okay with her. She wasn't really either. When she opened her eyes a bit later, there was a stranger in the room, and this one she didn't know. Without speaking to him, she reached down and pressed the nurse call button that she'd been handed the second time she woke.

"I'm not going to hurt you, and the nursing staff won't kick me out. Not without a fight." Thor didn't move as he stood up. "I'm Kaleb Jonas, a friend of Samuel's. I was with him when we came to save you."

The nurse walked in, and Thor glanced at her. She would never have believed it, but the man moved to the side of her bed in seconds and growled low. The nurse took a step back but didn't leave her.

"She called the desk." Kaleb glanced at her before looking back at the nurse. "We didn't know you were in here, Mr. Jonas. I'll let the others know."

"Wait." The nurse ran out of the room like she'd been shot from a gun and didn't stop when Thor tried to stop her. She looked at Kaleb and glared. "You need to get the fuck out of here."

"I don't think so. It's my turn to keep an eye on you." Thor didn't like the way he looked at her, like she was a morsel of chocolate and he was starved for something sweet. "You're healing nicely. I think that you should be up and about in a few more days."

"How long have I been here?" He told her thirteen days. "Mother fuck. I'm probably fired by now."

"I would doubt that. There's a manhunt out for you. They won't be able to find you, but they do continue to look. The mayor said you were a valued asset to the force and he wanted you found at all costs. Did you know that he's not human?" That question threw her, but she didn't have time to analyze what he meant. "Neither am I."

"Good for you. Who do I have to blow to get out of here?" His low growl this time made her skin pucker and her hair dance on her arms. Thor didn't have a clue why it made her want to touch him. "What is wrong with you?"

"You'll be blowing no one unless it's me. I'm not as possessive as some of the others in Samuel's pride, but I will kill any man you think to have sex with." Pride? Before she could get him to explain that, she felt someone coming toward them with ill intent. Kaleb moved to the foot of the bed and seemed to grow larger, which astounded her. He was already huge.

The man coming through the door wasn't anyone she knew, but apparently Kaleb did. Once the two of them seemed to come to some sort of silent agreement, they relaxed a little, enough for neither of them to go red on a second's notice. Going red was the way she felt about anger, and there was a great deal of that between these two men. They stepped back from each other a little more, but Kaleb didn't move from his position by her side, and the man seemed to think that was funny.

"You going to introduce me to her?" Kaleb didn't answer him and that had the other man laughing. "I'm not going to take her from you. I simply want to meet her."

"Why are you here?" The man's anger seemed to be there long enough for her to feel it. Then it disappeared. "I didn't tell you where I was, so what earthly reason can you have to be here?"

"I'm your brother. I think it only natural that I meet your mate. Don't you?" Thor could feel the way Kaleb felt about his brother, and it wasn't the warm and fuzzy feeling she thought siblings had for each other. When the other man started to step around Kaleb, he was suddenly across the room, hanging a foot from the floor.

"I didn't say you could come near her." Thor wanted to point out that she was right there and had been making all sorts of decisions on her own for years. But there was something more going on here, so she kept her mouth closed. This was not going to end well.

"Who is she?" When the man looked at her, she shrugged. There was no way she was telling this asshole who she was. He didn't like her. And for that reason alone, she didn't trust him. "Kaleb, I just want to meet your mate. Is that so bad?"

"Yes." Still holding his brother around the throat, Kaleb took him out of the room. She had no idea what happened on the other side of the closed door, but when Samuel came in frowning seconds later, she decided that she needed to get the hell out of there.

"Where are my clothes?" He didn't bother telling her that she wasn't healthy enough to leave the hospital, but pointed to one of the many cabinets on the wall. But getting to them proved to be something she wasn't sure she could do. "Help me?"

"I don't think so. Touching you right now could get me killed." Thor looked at the closed door, then at Samuel as he continued. "He might say he's not possessive, but he's a little on the pissed off side right now, and he might hurt me."

"Whatever." She tried again to get up, but all she managed to do was hurt herself. The scream that spilled from her mouth was out before she could stop it, and she found herself pressed back against the bed by Kaleb. This time his anger was directed at her.

"Stay still." She tried to brush him off, but he leaned down close to her ear and Thor felt herself wanting to bring him into the bed with her and wanting her gun at the same time. "I will join you there if you don't behave."

"Get out of here." He nipped her lobe, and she felt her body respond like he'd set her afire. Before she could do something stupid, like whimper, she curled her fingers into his hair and jerked him back. "I said to get out of here."

"I can smell you. You smell like sex." Suddenly, sex was all she could think about. When he kissed her throat, she did whimper then and looked into his eyes when he lifted his head. "We need to talk. Samuel said you have no idea what we are."

"Kaleb, perhaps this can wait." Kaleb stood up and looked at Samuel as he continued. She ignored them both, trying her best to get her breathing under control as well as her body. Looking down at herself, she realized that most of what had happened to her seemed to have healed too quickly.

"What the hell happened to me?" Both men looked at her. "And I don't mean at the big house. Why do I look like I've only had a slight accident and not someone cutting me to shit and back? Spill it."

Samuel flushed. She wasn't going to get anything from him unless she hurt him. And as much as she wanted answers, she wasn't up for taking him on right now. Instead, she looked at Kaleb. He didn't seem all that anxious to answer her, but he did sit down.

"How much do you remember?" Shivering, she didn't answer him, but he seemed to understand. "We found you from your connection to Samuel. When we got there, we had to take out a few of — "

"We who?" He grinned at her, and she had the sudden urge to smack the shit out of him. "If you called the police, you'd not be allowed in here. For that matter, where am I?"

"Pride Clinic. It's a private hospital that answers only to Samuel." Kaleb nodded to Samuel as her buddy sat down. "He owns this place and a few others. We answer to no one."

"So you're big cheese now. Good for you both. But that does not tell me how I managed to heal so quickly." When neither of them answered, she nearly told them to fuck off. But someone appeared in the room. And she knew that he didn't come through the fucking door.

~~~

Kaleb watched her closely. She was taking this better than he'd thought she would. She was a little freaked out when Stephen suddenly joined them, but she didn't scream or act all girly when he took a step toward her. Instead, she seemed to be reaching for a gun.

"Don't." Stephen stopped moving but smiled at her when she pulled her hand from her naked hip.

"What did you…how did you…? Fuck."

"Very good," he told her. Then Stephen looked at Kaleb. "You've bonded with her. You should know that I've made arrangements to have her moved to your home."

"Excuse me?" Everyone ignored Thor as Samuel spoke up.

"You have a home? Since when? I had no idea you even had anything but a cave you slept in on cold nights." Samuel grinned at him. "Can we see it? Is it one of those nice little places like Jimmy has? I hear the faeries are having fun with his place."

"I'm right here. Hello?" Kaleb looked at her but glared at Samuel.

"I have a real house and, no, you cannot see it. The faeries come to my house and I'll swat them away like flies. What's going on?"

"I've been informed that the scent she had on her was from a home close by. I think she's been touched by—" The shrill whistle had him put his hands over his ears. All of them looked at Thor, and Kaleb felt his boar stir, his bear. Christ, she looked good enough to eat.

"Now that I have your attention, I'd like to point out that I'm a grown woman—and I'm pretty sure it's silly of me to point this out—who has been on her own for more years than any of you morons have." Stephen snorted, but she ignored him. "As I was saying. I'm right here. Any and all decisions that you think to make for me or even about me will be cleared through me. I'm not a simpleton."

Both Samuel and Stephen looked at him. "She's right. She has been making her own decisions. As for her being a simpleton, I'm reasonably sure she's not that either."

"Thank you." Kaleb turned to look at her, and he could see that she was exhausted and took a step toward her. She put up her hand to stop him. "I want answers. Either you give them to me, or I swear to Christ the first time I have a gun back in my hand, I will shoot all three of you."

"Do you believe in vampires or shifters?" He watched her face for any sign that she was going to be upset, but she only shook her head at him. "I'm sorry to hear that. Stephen is a vampire. An old one as a matter of fact. I'm not sure how old, but with his age comes benefits that others wouldn't have. Such as his ability to be out in the daylight hours. Samuel is a shifter, as am I. He's a lion and the leader of this pride. He has a mate, as do I now. His mate is Kennedy. She, too, can shift, but she's a great deal more. How you doing?"

"And you? What are you?" He told her bear. "I see. And this would mean that...I'm guessing that as a vampire, he gave me his blood and healed me. It's why I'm in this sort of shape and not dead."

"He gave you blood at the scene of the crime, yes. But he didn't heal you. I did that." Again, Kaleb watched her face, and he could see that she wasn't afraid like he'd thought she might be, but a little confused. He waited for her to look at him again before he continued. "You're my mate. Do you know what that is?"

"No. And right now I have more questions about this scent and blood thing. Why did you give me blood?"

Stephen shifted on his feet, and she snapped her fingers at him. It was all Kaleb could do not to burst out laughing. "Answer me."

"I knew you were Samuel's friend, as he'd spoken about you before. As for giving my blood to you, it was to help you make it here so that we could put you back together." Stephen took a step toward her. "I do not appreciate you compelling me to answer you. Simply ask next time."

"Would you have answered me truthfully?" Stephen didn't answer her. She nodded. "I didn't think so. As for compelling you to answer me? I'm not sure what that means other than the true definition of the word. Are you saying I can make you answer me?"

"As I'm sure you can with most people."

She frowned at Stephen before looking at Kaleb. The connection was there for him to use, the one between mates. Kaleb thought if she could talk to Samuel that way, he would try as well.

"Do you have any idea what they'd done to you?" Without answering him verbally, she nodded. *"I'm going to kill the men who did this to you. All of them. And the man in charge. Do you know who it is?"*

"Yes." She answered him out loud, and Samuel looked at him as she spoke again. "I've always been able to talk to people through their mind. Samuel was the first one who ever spoke back to me. I think it had something to do with the head injury I had as a kid."

"It's more than that. You can compel and yes, it is just what it sounds like. I would imagine that it is the reason you've been so good at your job. You've made people tell you what you wanted to know." She shook her head, and Stephen nodded. "It is. And I'm pretty sure you know it.

Do the people you work for know anything about your abilities?"

"No, and I'd like to keep it that way." She looked at Kaleb. "You're not telling me the truth either, are you?"

"I'm not lying to you, but I want to speak to you before I talk to Samuel. There is a great deal more to me than anyone knows about." She nodded, then looked at Samuel.

"I need a place to stay. Do you have a hovel or something I can hide out in until I can figure out what's going on?" Kaleb felt Samuel look at him, but he watched her. She wasn't going to go easily. "I won't have you guys get into this any more. This shit I'm trying to bring in is not a nice guy."

"You can stay with me." She didn't acknowledge him, and he laughed. "Tania, if you go home with anyone else but me, I'll have to kill them."

Samuel stood up and patted him on the back. When he went to the door, Tania called him back, but he only stopped at the doorway as Stephen went out. Samuel looked at her.

"I'll be around if you need me. And you'll be in good hands with Kaleb. He won't let anyone hurt you." She was shaking her head when he laughed. "Christ, you're still as stubborn as you ever were, aren't you?"

"I can take care of myself. I do not need a sitter." Samuel was still laughing as he moved out of the room, and the door closed softly behind him. When she looked at Kaleb, he could see her anger. She was spitting mad. But Kaleb had to hand it to her. She was handling it much better than he would have.

"I'm your mate. I'm sworn to protect you above my own life." He watched her face when she leaned back on the bed and closed her eyes. "Tania, I can't make you go with me, but—"

"Don't call me that. My father calls me that, and I hate him more than I do you right now." She looked at him. "But you're coming in second really quick."

"I didn't mean to upset you." She only shook her head. "I want to tell you what I am. Then we can decide what to do about this situation you're in with your job."

"I'm really tired." He watched her open her eyes only to have them close again. "I need to rest, and I need for you to leave."

He sat very still, watching her until she was sleeping. Going to the door, he had a nurse bring her something for pain, and waited for twenty minutes before he reached into her sleeping mind to speak to her. But as soon as he reached into her mind, he found memories that made him think she was in more trouble than she'd realized. After sorting out the information he needed, he spoke to her to give her everything she might need.

"I've been touched by a witch in a way that makes me so much more than what I appear. Not even Stephen, with all his considerable age and magic, could come close to what I can do. I'm also a good deal older than I look. As of last month, I'm over two thousand years old. With that, like Stephen, I've grown more powerful. And as soon as we mate, you, too, will be just as strong." Her mind seemed to take this in, and he continued. *"The witch told me long ago that I'd meet you. I tried to tell her that I didn't want a mate, but she insisted that we'd be a value to each other. I've been waiting to tell you that I don't want you, but I've changed my mind. I need you."*

"No, you don't. You just think you do." He had to laugh. She was stubborn even in her subconscious. *"You should leave now before it's too late."*

"It's much too late for that. I've drank your blood and you've had mine." She shied away from that information, so he moved on. *"I'm a grizzly bear, changed when I helped someone with their child. It was what I needed at the time. My mother died when I was younger and left me with my brother, Langley."*

"And Langley? Why does he still live if this witch touched you and made you all that special?" It was a good question, one he had an answer for but was ashamed to tell her. *"You might as well spill it. I'm not going anywhere soon."*

"Has anyone ever told you you're like a dog with a bone?" She snorted at him, and he laughed. *"I will love to watch your face when I come deep inside of you. See what your breasts look like when I suckle hard at your nipples."*

"Never going to happen, and stop changing the subject." He laughed again and wondered if she would be this way when she was awake. *"I'm just me, Kaleb. A normal person that has been hurt way too many times by people to ever want to bring anyone into my life to be hurt again."*

"I'm not planning on hurting you. In fact, I'd very much like to work beside you when you take this man down." She mentioned his brother again. *"As I said, a dog with a bone. He was hurt long ago. Injured in what I had thought was someone else's doing. Turned out he'd been the bad guy and I saved him for naught. He's not a good person and if you must not trust anyone, he would be the one you should avoid at all costs."*

"I plan to avoid you as well. Whatever you think is going on between us must stop now. I'm not a very good person. And more than that, I work alone. It's all that has saved me all my life. Once I left Samuel, I was...." He felt her mind close off to him by degrees and was too impressed to remember he needed to talk to her before she nearly had him blocked out. *"You should leave."*

Kaleb watched her rest and wondered several things about her. First and foremost, who was this person named Sweeney that she'd just decided to investigate, and what did she mean about working alone? Did she really think that he'd let her go now? Kaleb leaned in and kissed her mouth gently. She tasted of warm air on a summer day and fall leaves at the same time. Standing up, he took her wrist to his mouth and bit down. Tasting her blood to make their connection stronger was what he told himself, but really, he just needed more of her with him.

"I'll be back, love." She moaned when he moved his mouth over her pounding pulse at her throat again. "When I do, you and I are going to get a start on this mating business. I've found that I have a powerful need to take you. And I need you healthy to do that."

He left her room and stopped by the desk to see the head nurse. After he left the clinic, he knew that no matter what, Tania…or Thor as she wanted to be called…would be well taken care of. As for anyone getting in to see or harm her, if anyone tried, they'd be met with a good deal more than they'd bargained for. Kaleb protected what was his.

Chapter 4

Lyod sat in Ansell's outer office for ten minutes before he realized that he'd been stood up. He wondered if the secretary knew that her boss was gone and was having a good laugh at his expense. Lyod decided that the next time she was out in her little red car, he was going to make sure she was pulled over for something. The bitch was going to pay for her little game. When the door opened and Ansell walked out, Lyod glanced at the woman again. She didn't even bat an eye at him as she handed Ansell some small pink slips. Lyod was motioned in, and he sat in a chair across the desk from Ansell.

"What have you found out?" Ansell put the messages on his desk, ignoring them as he spoke. "I haven't heard anything for a few days and the bitch has been out there for over two weeks."

"Nothing. And that could be a good thing. If she's not making any waves, she's either in a position where she can't or she's decided that it's too dangerous." Lyod didn't believe she'd just give up on this and was certain that she was dead. "I've had the hospitals and even the vets offices watched. She's never showed up at any of them. Whoever took her is long gone, too. Nothing on that front either."

"Except there has been movement from someone." Lyod frowned as Ansell continued. "Three of my men that were there that night are now missing or dead. The two that were found were torn up well beyond what was there at the compound. And the last one...well, I'm reasonably sure he was run through a wood chipper. His blood was found at the scene of one two nights ago."

"Fuck." Lyod tried to think. "Who would know who was there? I didn't have that list of names of those that came with you."

"Are you saying that I had something to do with this?" Lyod stood when Ansell did. His gun was currently in the front hall with his knife and badge. Ansell, however, had his gun pointed right at him. "You should think very hard before you answer that."

"No. What I meant was, I have no way of seeing to the men who were there. I have no list so that I can keep an eye on them. I'm not blaming anyone, but would very much like to get a handle on this before anyone else comes up missing." Lyod sat down when Ansell did, but the gun now laying on the desk made him nervous. "I have a man missing, too. If your men are coming up missing, I can only assume that a few of mine might as well. Do you think she's trying to flush us out into the open?"

"How should I know what goes through the mind of someone like her? You told me she was unstable at best, and now she's not only been to my house, but killed several of my men before we were able to take her. She sounds like someone I should have hired instead of you."

Lyod hated Thornton now more than ever. She'd made him look like a fool. "I'm controllable, and she's not. Hell, I couldn't get her to listen to me if I tried. She had her own set of rules that she went by and fucked me up all the time." Of course, they were the rules that all of them were supposed to follow, but Lyod had never been one to do that. Instead, he liked to be the one who made the rules. That way he could change them as it suited him. But never Thornton. She had to do things by the book, always by the fucking book.

"I want you to continue looking for her. If you don't have her in some way or fashion, and I mean dead or alive, I'll have to take other measures." Ansell glanced at the gun before continuing. "She's seen my face, knows where I live. What will you do when she knows the same about you?"

A threat. A good one, too. Lyod didn't say anything because he was trying to think how much damage she'd do to him if she only knew a third of what he'd been doing since he'd been on the force. And even a drop of what he'd done since she'd been working for him. Lyod was fucked either way. And he knew then that he'd have to find her on his own if for no other reason than he could kill her for fucking up his perfect life. Nodding to Ansell, he stood up.

"I'll find her. I'll do it myself if need be. And once I do, I'll kill her for you and bring you her head." Ansell smiled and told him there was no reason for that. "You'll know that I've done my job as soon as it's complete."

"See that I do." Lyod was nearly to the door of the office when Ansell said his name. Turning, he looked at him. "You'll regret this if you think to turn me in to save your own ass. I will mess you up in ways that will make what my men did to her look like a small scrape. Do I make myself perfectly clear?"

"Yes, sir. I understand." Lyod retrieved his gun and badge from the silent man at the door before going out to his car. He sat there for several minutes before he started the engine and pulled out into the street. As far as threats went, Lyod knew that Ansell would follow through on everything he'd said. But what Lyod feared most was Thornton getting wind of what his involvement had been in everything that he and Ansell had been doing. She would not only bury him, but she'd put him in front of a firing squad. Or get him hanged. Lyod knew that either way, he was as dead as he hoped she was.

Lyod went home. There was no reason for him to go back to the office, so he pulled into his driveway a few minutes later. He was surprised to see a limo parked in front of his house. Getting out, he nearly got back into his car when he saw who the driver was.

"Gilbert? What are you doing here?" Lyod's ex-wife had been told repeatedly not to come here without an invitation. It seemed she did what she wanted when she wanted, and he'd had enough. Hearing her screaming at someone at the top of her lungs, he went into the house without waiting for an answer from the driver. He found Sheila arguing with his butler.

"I will not wait outside. I've come here to get my things he owes me or else." She turned on him the moment she saw him. "Where the hell are they? I want them right fucking now, or so help me I'll have my lawyers come here and get them."

"It might help me to tell you if I had any idea what you were talking about." Lyod handed his briefcase to his butler, and the man ran off with it as if he'd been handed a bomb and needed to dispose of it. He supposed in a way he had. Sheila was a fucking time bomb every time she came there. "What are you doing here? I think you've been told many times that this place is no—"

"I want my diamonds." He smiled at her. "You said I could have them, and I want them. Now. I need them."

"Your diamonds? How do you figure that they belong to you? If I remember correctly, and for the record I do, you were given all you were supposed to have months ago. And the diamonds, because of their value to me, were not on the list of things you got. You'll not get them to sell off for something trivial. Or is it more debt, Sheila? I thought for sure once the divorce was settled, you would understand that you need to pay your own bills. I'm not going to be footing them forever." She snarled, and Lyod laughed. "Are you upset about something?"

"You motherfucker, you cut off my credit cards, and I no longer have access to the checking account. Half of that money is mine." Lyod laughed and walked by her to the den. He needed a drink. "Give me my diamonds now and I'll forget the other jewels I left behind."

"You mean when I kicked you out. No, I don't think so. I never said I'd give them to you after I caught you fucking everything that had a dick. Besides, I more than deserve them for all the shit I had to put up with from you." He took a long drink of his bourbon before looking at her. "And as for you having half my checking account, whatever gave you that idea? I think you should read the decree again. I owe you nothing."

"I don't fucking have any money. How the hell am I supposed to live on the little money you paid me for the lawyer fees?" She advanced toward him, and he simply moved his coat so that she could see that he was still armed. "You'd shoot me?"

"Yes. In a heartbeat." He moved to sit on the couch, and she stood there. Lyod was trying to remember why he ever thought she was going to be a good wife. The few years they'd been married had soured him on ever finding himself a wife ever again. Sheila moved to sit down, and he shook his head. "I think it's time you left. And when you're home again, I would suggest you try to figure out a bus schedule. I will call to have you taken off Gilbert's to-do list as soon as you're gone."

"You bastard." Lyod nodded at her description of him. "Why are you doing this? We got along all right, didn't we?"

"I suppose in your little mind we did. You fucked everyone you wanted, and I provided a home for you to turn your tricks in. I no longer want you in my life. And as of right now, you come here again and I'll make sure you never bother anyone ever again." Lyod watched her try to regain control of her temper. Christ, he might be having the best time he'd ever had with her since he'd fucked her the first time. "Don't come here again, Sheila, or so help me, you'll regret it."

"I know things about you." He didn't bother asking her what she thought she might know. There was nothing. She was a liar now and always would be to get what she wanted. "I can go to your little boss and tell him what you've been up to. I know things."

"You know nothing or you would have told your lawyer before the final divorce. And what you think you know will never fly. I will end you before you get to tell one person." She looked around the room, and he watched her. She'd been violent that last time she'd been here, and he would really shoot her if she tried that shit again. "Try it. Come on, try it please."

"I hate you." He nodded and took another drink as she stood up. "I really do hate you and will find a way to make you pay for this. I deserve more than what you settled on me. Five hundred thousand dollars isn't enough."

He watched her for several seconds and then laughed. "You're broke, aren't you? You've already blown through all that money and now you want more. You fucking idiot. What do you plan to do now?"

"Oh, you will give me more, and if not, I'll find another sucker. But this time I'll be more careful not to get caught." She moved toward the door, and he got up to follow her. When she turned suddenly, he moved his hand toward his gun and stilled. "You really would shoot me, wouldn't you?"

"As I've said before, in a heartbeat." He led her to the door and nearly shoved her out onto the front steps. "Don't come back here. I swear if you do, you'll never leave in one piece."

Sheila stomped to the car and got in. When Gilbert looked up at him, Lyod gave him the thumbs up. Tomorrow he'd be unemployed, but he was reasonably sure the man would thank him for it. Closing the door, Lyod went to his office. It was time to find the little cunt.

~~~

She was going stir crazy. Thor knew that if she had to watch any more television, she was going to kill someone. Who had time to make this shit up? And when the next show was another one about court cases, she turned it off. Enough was enough. The door opening had her reaching for the gun that wasn't there.

"Do you do that every time someone comes to visit you?" Samuel handed her a large bag with grease stains on the outside of it. "You tell anyone where you got that and I'll never bring you another thing."

The smell was enough to make her drool and when she opened the bag, she looked at Samuel with tears in her eyes. "You remembered."

He nodded and smiled at her. There had been no money when they'd been children. Not even enough to go to get a burger between them. And they would talk about all the things they were going to do when they had some extra cash. She had wanted to get a supersized burger meal with fries and a milk shake. When the tall frosty glass was set beside her food, she reached for his hand.

"Samuel, I'm so glad we're friends. You've no idea how many times over the years I would think of you and smile. Think of all the promises we made to each other and how we would escape our lives." He nodded and kissed her hand. "Thank you."

"You're very welcome. And there are times when I was trying to make a decision about a business deal and I'd find myself wondering what you'd do. Most of the time thinking of you and what you'd tell me was dead on. And when it wasn't, it was damned close. You're the best friend a guy could have." He moved to the chair while she devoured the burger and fries. She knew that there was more that he wanted to say to her, but she was glad that he was waiting until she was finished eating. When the nurse came in while she was finishing up, she only smiled and took her blood pressure. Apparently, Samuel did have a lot of pull here.

"I have to talk to you." He nodded at her after the meal was gone and the mess was cleaned up. "I have to get going. My boss is more than likely looking for me."

She knew he might be, but she wasn't really in any hurry to let him find her. There were a few things that had happened that night that she was still wondering about.

Like how did all those extra men know to come out when she'd been talking to Sweeney? And why did he seem pissed that she'd gone to the house instead of standing down like he'd told her to do?

"I don't think that's such a good idea. I know that you're good at your job. I've looked you up, but you're supposed to be dead, not running around like a maniac trying to bring some asshole in. Rest for a while." She started shaking her head. "Don't do that. I need you to be around for a little while longer. My son will be born soon, and I want you here to meet him."

"If they find me here, and I've no doubt that they will, your son might be hurt. Do you want that?" He stood up and started to pace. She waited to see if he'd tell her she was right. They both knew that she was, but he had to admit it or he'd never let her go. "Samuel?"

"I'm really a werelion, Thor. I know you probably don't really believe me, but we're all something extra. Something that can help protect you from this man." She shook her head again, not believing he was still trying to tell her this. "Shall I show you?"

"Show me what? That you think you're something more than a man? You don't really believe that, do you? I mean come on, Samuel, this is me you're talking to." The room tightened a little, and she looked around. Something was— "Mother fuckballs."

Samuel was gone. Not gone, she supposed, but no longer who she thought he should have been. When the large lion walked slowly to her bed, she moved back as far as she could and watched him. If he bit her right now, she'd be dead. Not from the bite but from the massive heart attack she was going to have.

"I told you so." She looked at him when he touched her mind and spoke. *"And the rest of us are what we said as well."*

"I'm dreaming." He leapt up onto the bed and laid down at the foot. "Please don't eat me. I believe you. Christ, I believe you."

"I'm going to change back now. Will you be all right while I go out?" She nodded. *"You'll have to open the door for me."*

She started to stand up to let him out and then lock the door after him when Kaleb walked in. He stared at her, then at Samuel before he held the door open wide. Samuel jumped from the bed and to the floor in a fluid motion that had her nearly asking him to do it again. But fear of what she was seeing made her snap her mouth closed. She only just realized she wasn't alone when she heard the click of the lock as Kaleb shut the door.

"I see he had to convince you." She nodded, not sure what was really going on. "Are you all right?"

She nodded, then shook her head. "No, I'm not fucking all right. He just changed into a lion. Right here. What the fuck is up with that?"

"I could change into a bear if it would make you forget about him being a lion." He said this with all seriousness that had her looking at him hard. "You believe I'm a bear yet?"

"Why are you doing this to me? All of you? I've been all right in the head until now. Could it be that I've been in a coma all this time and you guys aren't real?" He smiled and sat on the bed next to her. "I'm wide awake, aren't I?"

"You are." He leaned forward just enough that he was a whisper from her mouth. "You're very much wide awake. Can I kiss you? I'd very much like to taste what you're keeping from me."

"I don't think so. I don't have anything special. I'm just me." Her voice sounded like she'd been running after a perp. When she cleared her throat to try again, he brushed his mouth over hers so softly that she moaned slightly. "I thought I said no."

"Your mouth says no, but your scent says to taste. I'm going to kiss you, Thor. Will you let me in?" Let him in? Christ, she wanted to let him have her, but this was a bad idea. But before she could tell him the million and one reasons why he shouldn't kiss her, he cupped his hand into the back of her head and pulled her to him.

His mouth was soft and firm at the same time. Kaleb moaned when she allowed him to swirl his tongue against hers, and she knew the moment he pulled her into his lap that this was going to go way beyond him simply kissing her. Putting her hands onto his chest to push him away, she found herself curling her fingers into his shirt and hanging on. Good Christ, this man could kiss. As soon as her back touched the bed, he lifted his head.

"I want you." She wasn't sure if she could say no because her entire body was screaming at her to tell him yes. "Let me taste you. Just enough so that I can take you with me for the rest of the day."

The snaps of her gown opening sounded loud in the room. Kaleb never took his eyes from hers as he pulled each one free and slowly peeled the material down. When the coolness of the room made her realize that she was bared to him, she started to put her hand over herself.

"Don't. Let me look at you." His eyes traveled down her body to her chest, and she felt her body tighten. "Lovely. More than lovely, you're exquisite."

Taking his time, he leaned down to her breast and licked the tip. Her nipple puckered so tightly that it was almost painful. But when Kaleb took her into his mouth, suckling on just her hard peak, Thor wrapped her hand into his hair and pulled him tighter.

Nothing could have prepared her for the feelings, the sensations, or the overwhelming need she felt at that moment. When he shifted on the bed, settling between her thighs so that he was over her, Thor knew that if he wasn't inside of her soon, she'd simply come while he ground against her.

"I'm not going to last much longer." He chuckled at her, and she moaned when he bit into her breast. "I need you."

"I can smell your need. Can I drink from you? Taste your nectar as you come down my throat?" Nodding, she nearly cried out when he sat up and stood near the bed. "I'm going to make you scream."

"Please. Hurry." He nodded and reached for the chair behind him. Pulling it to the edge of the bed, she moved to sit down, not really sure what he was doing. As soon as he sat before her and opened her legs to settle on either side of his body, she leaned back. Thor could feel her juices as they poured from her.

"Come for me when you want. I want to drink my fill." She didn't think she'd have any problem coming. He lifted her hips up enough to cup her ass, and she nearly cried out when he tore her panties from her. "Christ, you smell delicious."

But instead of taking her, he stood suddenly. Both of them looked to the door when the handle turned. The low growl from him had her body go on high alert. Someone was trying to get in.

"*Don't move.*" She nodded at his command as he moved her legs from around him. When he kissed her calf before putting it on the bed, she looked up at him. "*They smell like someone that was at the compound. I have to check it out.*"

"*The door is locked.*" He nodded at her and smiled. "*You're going to go out there, aren't you?*"

"*Yes. As much as I'd like to finish what we've started here, I think it best to do it where you're safe and we will be free of interruptions.*" He slid his fingers over her breast to her core. She moaned when he slid inside of her. "*They're going to release you today. Come to my house with me. I want to see you naked in my bed.*"

"*I can't stay with you. I have to get back to my job.*" He moved his fingers in and out of her, touching her clit with every move. "*Please, you're killing me. Either make me come or go. I can't —*"

The door rattled on its hinges. Kaleb moved to the door and stood with his back to it. She watched as he licked her juices off his fingers. Every cell in her body could feel it. When he motioned for her to cover up, she did so.

Someone was coming in whether she wanted them to or not.

Chapter 5

Kaleb reached over and unlocked the door as quietly as he could. The man on the other side was going to be surprised when he came into this room. Kaleb glanced at the bed to see that not only had Thor redressed, but she was also standing there with a silver IV pole in her hand. Christ, the woman looked like a warrior. And he wanted to go over to her, press her to the wall, and fuck her until neither of them could stand.

The door opened slowly, and when the man slipped into the room with his gun out, Kaleb knocked the gun away and put his hand around the man's neck. It snapped before he could think to hold back on his strength. The man now hung limply in his hand.

"You killed him?" Kaleb looked at Thor and nodded. "Are you kidding me? How the fuck do we find out who sent him now? Damn it. Have you ever heard of waiting?"

"I was still hyped up about fucking you." She glared at him, but he wanted to smile. This woman was adorable when she was pissed. But he wisely didn't tell her that. "I didn't mean to kill him. Believe it or not, I wanted to question him, too."

"Well that's fucking not going to happen now, is it?" She put the pole down, for which he was thankful. He thought she looked ready to commit her own murder. "I guess we'll have to call the police."

"I don't think that would be such a good idea." Kaleb had put the man down on the floor and was searching his pockets. When he handed her the badge, she stared at it for a long time before looking up at him. "Do you know this man?"

Her head shook slowly before she finally spoke. "He works in the same house that I do. The same police station. But I've never seen him before."

He didn't want to alarm her, but they needed to get her out of there now. He reached for Samuel and told him what had happened. The man said he'd be there in a few minutes; he was still in the hospital. Samuel thought the same thing he did...they needed to get her to a safe place. Before he could speak to her, she started talking.

"I knew something was wrong that night. When Sweeney told me that I should stand down, I was confused. He'd been hounding me to let this go for months, and when I finally found the man, he said that he'd look into it for me. Then I was talking to him and he was pissed that I was there. I think he sent the others out to kill me." Kaleb let her talk while he pulled her clothes from the small dresser and handed her things to put on. When she didn't seem to be making any progress with it, he pulled her gown off and hurriedly dressed her.

"I'm in trouble here." He nodded at her while he buttoned her shirt. "They're going to find me and when they do, whoever is with me will go down as well. I need to get away now."

"The only place you're going is to my house. No one will get on my property without getting themselves killed." She didn't answer him but did take her pants from him when he handed them to her. "Thor, honey, you have to hurry. There might be more than just him here. Samuel is making a sweep of the hospital, but we have to get you to somewhere safe."

"Do you have my gun? If not, do you know who does?" The tightening of the room was all the warning they had before Stephen and Vinnie were there. Vinnie handed her a large handgun, and Stephen picked up the dead man. "Are you going to take him to the morgue?"

"No." Stephen looked at him before speaking to Thor. "You need to get to Kaleb's house. There are at least three other humans in this building that we don't know."

"I need to fill out a statement. It was self-defense." She looked at Vinnie before she continued, and Kaleb felt sorry for her. "What the fuck do you think is so funny? Let me guess, you're a lion, too."

"Nope. Dragon." She took a step back and backed right into him. Kaleb told Vinnie to behave. "I'm being very nice. When Samuel called me, I was in the middle of a huge project. I'm a little on the tense side. I don't care for humans on the whole, and cops I hate."

When Thor took a step toward Vinnie, Kaleb stopped her by pulling her back. "We don't really have time for a large debate here. When this is all over, you two can talk your differences over, and I'll patch up the winner."

"You think he can take me?" He glanced at Vinnie, who winked at him. Kaleb knew then what he'd been doing. Kaleb could already feel that the tension in her was less. "I'm pretty sure I can take him."

"You think?" Vinnie looked her up and down and grinned. "Maybe, but when you come to fight me, perhaps you should button your shirt better. You'll distract me this way."

When Kaleb turned her around, he realized that without a bra on, she was pretty exposed to them, and the fact that he hadn't buttoned her shirt properly caused most of her creamy flesh to be exposed. And the nice little suckle mark that he'd given her was right there in the opening. Thor smacked his hands away when he reached for her to redo them.

"I've got it. Damn it all to hell." The door moving had them all turning, and he nearly shoved her behind him when he realized he might get shot if he did. Her gun was pointed right at the door about where a heart would be on a man if he came in. Kaleb lowered her gun when he heard Samuel speak.

"We have to move. Now," Samuel said as he moved into the room.

"I'm taking you to my house." She nodded at him, and he pulled her to him. A quick kiss to her mouth had her standing there looking at him until he closed her mouth. She glared.

"I'm not having sex with you." He simply nodded at her when she continued to stand there. "I mean it. I had a small loss of my senses, but I'm okay now."

"You and I are going back to my house, and I'm taking you right to bed. Once I have you there, I'm going to make love to you all the rest of the day and mostly through the night." When Samuel cleared his throat, Kaleb realized that they weren't alone. He'd completely forgotten about everything when he touched her. "Ready?"

Thor stood there for several seconds. He was sure she was trying to figure out if he was talking about them in bed or was she ready to leave. As soon as he got her home, he'd show her just how persuasive he could be. As they moved through the hospital and to the waiting car out front, she never spoke to him, but she didn't really need to. He could feel her turmoil as if it were his own. They were bonded now.

The ride to his house was made mostly in silence. When she spoke, it was to answer a question someone asked her, but for the most part she ignored him. Kaleb was fine with that for now. She was a tad overwhelmed.

"The man you stopped, did you know him?" Samuel looked at him when she didn't answer right away. "Thor, did you know him?"

"He worked at the same house I did. I didn't know him, but…. I need for you to pull over. I'm going to be sick." As soon as the words left her mouth, the driver pulled over. Kaleb helped her out, and she ran to the bushes just off the road. He started toward her when she touched his mind. *"They're going to kill you. I don't need more deaths on my head."*

"He can try. I can't die. And neither can you, I'm pretty sure." And he'd be surer of that answer when they mated. She would be his in all ways. *"Are you okay now?"*

"No, I'm not fucking okay. Do you know that he came in there to kill me? To do just what his boss…my boss told him to do?" Kaleb paused when he realized she could read minds. *"What the fuck am I supposed to do now? Go back to my job and pretend that nothing happened? I don't think that's going to work out."*

"Probably not." He waited for her to come out and pulled her into his arms when she started toward the car again. "I keep telling you this, and maybe sometime you'll believe me, but I can protect you. I can help you protect both of us."

"You're not going to let me go, are you?" Kaleb didn't bother answering her when she pulled away from him. "I'm going to get killed trying to protect you all, and there isn't a damned thing I can do about it. And I'm not going to have sex with you."

"You keep telling yourself that. But when I get you home, I'm going to enjoy showing you just how quickly you're going to change your mind." He watched her face and was surprised by the need he saw there. Then he stepped toward her and yanked her to him. Her scent drove him hard, and he crushed his mouth over hers.

His own need spiraled out of control. Picking her up by her ass, he moaned when she wrapped her legs around his waist and her arms around his neck. Now, he needed her right now.

Stepping toward the group of trees just in front of him, he pressed her back to the first one he came to and tore his mouth from hers to nip at her throat. Tearing open her shirt, he took her breast into his mouth and suckled hard at her as he tried to untangle her pants from her.

"You're going to rip them." Kaleb growled at her and did just what she said. "Fuck, you're going to tear me apart. Hurry."

His pants were suddenly undone, and she reached into them to wrap her hand around him. It was all he could do not to come all over her. Rocking into her hand, he tried to tell himself to slow down, but she was making it extremely difficult. As soon as she was naked, he lifted her again and slammed deep inside of her even as he took her scream into his mouth.

Tasting her tears had him still all movement. Lifting his head, Kaleb looked down at her and felt his heart twist. He'd hurt her—and badly if the pain in her eyes was any indication. Kissing her gently, he pulled her to his heart and held her.

"I'm sorry." She mumbled something that he didn't understand but nodded at her. Kaleb told her over and over how sorry he was. He heard movement behind them and growled low.

"*Go the fuck away.*" Kaleb heard Stephen laugh and wanted to go to him and tear his face off. "*I'm seriously going to kill you when we meet again.*"

"*I was told to make sure the two of you were all right. I'm assuming you are.*" Kaleb was trying to think of a polite way to tell him to fuck off when he continued. "*I'm going to tell them you're going to make your own way home. You're not far from your house, are you?*"

"No." Thor shifted in his arms and looked up at him. Kaleb felt his heart fill with her. "*Stephen, do you suppose we're supposed to fall in love with our mates as quickly as this?*"

"*I don't know, man. I've already decided that my mate and I missed the boat somehow.*" There was a long pause, and then he spoke again. "*I'm leaving you to this. Let me know if you need anything.*"

"They're going to leave us here." He nodded at Thor, and she shifted. "You're still very hard."

"I am." He kissed her mouth gently and rocked into her before he could think not to. "And you are very tight. I'm sorry that I hurt you."

"Please do that again." He moved harder this time, making his cock ache to take her again and again. "Kaleb, please. You've been teasing me all day. Give it to me."

Lifting her higher, he took her nipple into his mouth as he filled her over and over. Sweat streamed down his spine as he tried to be as gentle as he could. But she wasn't making it easy for him. When she scraped her teeth over his shoulder, he wanted to beg her to bite him, but she leaned back and looked at him.

"I've never come before." Kaleb nodded. "I think if I don't very soon, I might hurt you. Do you have any idea how much I hurt right now?"

Rolling his hips, she moaned. He then slowed his movements. When she dug her nails into his skin, Kaleb smiled and pulled her feet from around him. Her whimper had him nearly take her again, but he had a better idea.

"I'm going to eat you." Taking a step back, he held her still until she was steadier on her feet. "Then, when I've had my fill, I'm going to fuck you hard and fast, filling you with my cum over and over. Will that be all right with you?"

Dropping to his knees before her, he pulled her hips toward him. She smelled of sex and her own juices. Her blood was there, too, just a smear on her thighs, and he licked it off her. Sliding his hand up her thigh, he moved his finger deep into her pussy and felt her tightness again.

"Please, Kaleb. Please?" He leaned in and took her hard nubbin into his mouth and nipped as he fucked her slowly with his fingers. Licking her from gate to clit, he gathered as much of her juices on his tongue as he could and moaned at her taste. Suckling her clit into his mouth again, he felt her fingers curl into his hair, and she held him to her. Kaleb brought her to a quick and loud climax almost immediately.

"Again. Come again, love." She did. Over and over, she flooded his mouth with her essences. Every time she begged him to stop, he doubled his efforts to bring her again. When her knees began to tremble, he pulled her to the ground and leaned over her, fisting his cock.

"When I enter you, I'm going to mark you in a way that will bond us forever." She nodded. "You'll be my mate in all ways. We'll never be parted. We'll belong only to each other."

"If you don't do something soon, forever won't be as long as you think it should." Laughing, he moved over her and lifted her legs up so that they rested over his shoulder. Her pussy was right where he wanted her, and he leaned over her and slowly entered her.

There was no pain this time, he knew. But he still went slowly, moving in and out of her until he was sure she could take him. Sliding her legs to his hips, Kaleb settled between her legs and took her mouth. He was so close to coming that he knew that when he did, she wasn't going to get anything from this.

Cupping her ass, he brought her up tighter against him and brushed against her tight hole. When she moaned, Kaleb slid his finger into her and watched her shatter beneath him.

"Again. Come for me again, love." She bowed up off the ground and screamed out her release. Kaleb buried his face into her shoulder and bit her as his own release took him. The connection between them was profound. When her body began to ramp up for another powerful climax, Kaleb felt it, and his body responded accordingly. As soon as she came again, screaming out his name, Kaleb threw back his head and roared out his climax. *Christ*, he thought, *I'm in love with her.*

~~~

"I've not heard from Camp, have you?" His assistant shook his head and pulled out a file. Lyod took it from him but didn't open it. "Where was he going?"

"He and Archer found out about this clinic on Tenth. They took Sams and were headed over there about two hours ago. He's not supposed to check in for another hour." Lyod nodded and headed to his office, telling him to let him know when he heard anything.

He dropped the file at his desk as he sat down. And still no word about the fucking cunt. He had no idea where she was and worse yet, he didn't have a clue where else to look for her. It was as if she'd dropped off the earth. His phone ringing had him look at the caller ID before he picked it up. Pausing just long enough, he was glad when it finally stopped ringing. He didn't want to have to deal with anyone right now, especially Ansell. Leaning back in his chair, he thought of the last meeting he'd had with him.

~~~

"Did you find her?" Sadly, he told him no. "Well, you have five days to find her or I do something to make sure that my name is not connected with your department and the girl. I'll make sure that no one knows a fucking thing."

Lyod still wondered how he was going to perform that miracle but didn't ask. He was sort of afraid of the answer. All sorts of things came to mind and none of them had him living for very long.

"I have my best men on it. The mayor has an entire team set up to take calls and go out on leads. Which I might add is very little. But we're looking, and I'm looking. I've gone to her house and no one has been there in—"

"I don't give a fuck where you've looked. It's not in the right places, so shut up about them." Ansell started pacing. "Someone is looking into my business. I don't know who yet but whoever it is, they've got more than they should have. I'm thinking this person works for someone very powerful and they know where she is."

He started to ask him if he had an IP address but didn't want to have to explain to him again what the Internet protocol was. No matter how many times he'd explained it to him over the years, the man simply never got it.

"I'll talk to your IT guys and see if we can set up something that might backfire on them." Ansell nodded but didn't say much more. Instead of waiting for the silence to end, Lyod told him what he'd been able to find out about the girl. Most of it was things he felt he should have been told before he had to hire her.

"Did you know that at one time she worked as a Secret Service guard for the president? She'd been in the service, too. Probably some dyke that had to get out when she made a pass at some broad." He laughed a little at his own joke and looked up when Ansell sat down.

"She retired from the SS about five years ago. About the time she came to work for you. And as for her being a dyke, she's not. At least not that anyone knows. As far as anyone can tell, she's simply not interested in anything but advancing her career. And she's done a fucking good job at that, too." Ansell pointed to a file. "You should read some of the shit she's done. Fucking honor student in school. Graduated top of her class at Brown, and she's been nominated, by your own men, for the Mayoral Award he gives out for distinguished service every year.

She's won three times out of five. You should take better care to find out about those who work for you."

~~~

After that, the meeting had centered on how incompetent he was. How he'd let this woman, his own employee, get the better of both of them. And worse yet, how even with all his men, all the equipment in the world at his fingertips, he'd still managed not to find one fucking female. And to a point it was true.

But Lyod could hardly go out to the bullpen, what the men called their meeting place, and tell them that he thought maybe Thornton had witnessed him dallying with a known criminal and she'd gotten herself hurt pretty bad. And now he and this criminal element couldn't find her. Then he would order them to hit the streets, find her for them, and kill her dead. Yeah, he thought, that'd go over really well.

"Sir, you might want to turn on the news. I think there's been an accident." Dreading this more than the phone call, he picked up the remote and turned on the television like his assistant suggested. And there on the screen were pictures of two of his men, Sams and Archer. Turning up the volume, he listened to what had happened to them.

"About two hours ago, the police pulled this man's body from the river and in the truck they discovered the grisly remains of a third man who has yet to be identified. This man, John Archer, was driving the car when it entered the river. A third man, Paul Sams, was apparently ejected from the car and his body was found deeper in the river by divers. It is unknown if the third man knew the other two but for now, we have three dead men." He looked at Kolby when his phone rang. Neither of them went to answer it.

"Do you suppose the last man is Camp?" Lyod nodded and turned off the television. "Who do you suppose would have done that to them? You don't think that they simply killed each other and stuffed Camp in the trunk, do you?"

"How the fuck should I know." Lyod sat down hard. "Mother fuck, this woman is driving me crazy. Go down there and see what you can find out. And for Christ's sake, put the phones on service. I don't want to have to try and explain this to Ansell."

When he was gone, Lyod gathered up his things and decided to go home. This wasn't a place to be if he didn't want to talk to Ansell. By the time he was pulling out of the long parking lot of his private offices, he saw a limo pulling in. Smiling for the first time in days, he made his way home to hide and plan. Things were going south in a big fat hurry.

Chapter 6

After rolling out of the unfamiliar bed, Thor stood there looking around for several seconds before someone made a soft noise beside her. She looked down at the man who lay there sleeping. Christ, he was fucking huge. Blushing furiously, she made her way to the bathroom.

Turning on the shower after using the toilet, she looked at herself in the mirror as the steam filled the room. She'd had sex with a man who claimed he was a bear. And her best friend was a lion. Wiping the steam away as it blurred her appearance, she decided to stop thinking about them and focus on what she was up to.

"Nothing." Her voice didn't echo in this bathroom like it did in her own. There was tile in here, earth tones that set the style for the bedroom, too. Wondering how she got off track again, she stepped into the spray and moaned. This was what a lot of water pressure felt like.

Thor thought of Sweeney and knew that somehow he was in on what had gone down at Lipscomb's house. She wasn't sure how yet, but she'd get there. Washing her hair with Kaleb's shampoo, she felt her body react strongly to his scent. "Damn it. Focus."

"Do you always talk to yourself in the shower? If so, you might want to try a little positive talk. Cursing at yourself isn't a good way to start your day." Thor watched as the door to the stall opened slowly and he was there. "Good morning. Would you mind very much if I joined you?"

She was shaking her head before she could think of several hundred reasons why she should shower alone. When he stepped from around the door and into the hot water with her, all thoughts of him not joining her fled. And when he reached for her, she went to him willingly.

The kiss was gentle. For a man his size, she'd been surprised by how gentle he could be with everything he did to her. Blushing again, she tried to pull away, but he held her tightly. Thor felt his cock thicken at her belly.

"You're not very talkative to other people in the morning, are you? That's okay. I can do it for you until you get your feet under you. What would you like to do today? I was thinking we'd mess up the bed more before going down and eating a hearty breakfast. That way I'd have more energy for when I bring you back up here and eat you."

When she pulled back this time, he let her. "Is having sex all we're going to ever do? Don't answer that. I have to get to my things. I'm pretty sure that my house is being watched now that I've figured out that Sweeney is in on this, whatever *this* is."

"I can get your things for you without anyone knowing. Stephen owes me and...why are you shaking your head?" Thor grabbed the large sea sponge and raked it over her body while she tried to think how to answer him.

"He says he's a vampire. While I don't really know if he is or not, I'm not really into owing him. Will his payment be a gallon of my blood? Will he make me have sex with him?" She looked at him when he growled. "Oh, so you get all possessive now? Grow up. I'm talking out loud. It's the way I work. Where was I?"

"Sex with Stephen. Which isn't going to happen, and he won't bite you without permission. By the way, you have some of his blood, so he can hear you when you speak to him." Kaleb took the sponge from her and filled it with his soap. "Turn around and I'll wash your back while you think."

She didn't have a clue how that was supposed to work. Whenever he touched her, she melted. While she loved him touching her and the whole melting thing, she wasn't in the mood to get distracted again.

"He somehow knew that I was there. I'm not sure if he was actually there or not, but I'm willing to bet he was somewhere close. Why would he tell me to look into the drugs and where they were coming from if he was in on it? Unless he didn't know that Lipscomb had anything to do with this." She moaned when Kaleb had her brace her hands on the tiled wall while he massaged her shoulders. "Christ, I could get used to this."

"If you think Sweeney is part of this Lipscomb thing, how many do you suppose work with you and for him?" Good question, and she told him so. "I used to be a cop in one of my lives."

"One of your lives?" She moaned again when he pressed his body to hers. "You've said you're older than you look. How old are you...I mean, exactly how old are you?"

"Old. I want to taste you." Without waiting for her to answer him, assuming she could at this point, he turned her around and dropped to his knees in front of her. "I'm nearly as old as Stephen. We knew each other before he changed. I'm going to enjoy this."

Kaleb pulled her toward him and buried his face in her pussy. When he nipped at her clit as he slid his fingers inside of her, Thor held onto the wall. Right now she didn't care if he was a thousand years old. The things he did to her made her scream.

Her climax was quick and when he lifted his head from her, she thought he was satisfied. Christ, was she ever wrong. Lifting her leg so that it rested on his shoulder, he lifted her up by her ass and suckled her pussy into his mouth. When he entered her with his tongue, she cried out and wrapped her fingers into his hair to hold on.

He ate her. She'd never been so close to paradise so many times only to be held off from going over the edge into it. And begging him didn't work. When she was ready to kill him or slide her fingers into herself and get the satisfaction he was denying her, he stopped.

"I need you." She nodded. When he stood up and pulled her to his body, she felt his muscles. His chest hair brushed against her nipples, making them painfully aware of him. The shower was suddenly off, and she stood holding onto him, trembling.

"If I take you now, I'll harm you. I should have...I need to mate with you. Do you know what that means?" Thor told him she didn't, not really. "It means that we have to exchange blood with a bite. I need to mark you in a way of my kind. I need to hurt you."

"Hurt me?" He nodded, and that's when she noticed how terrified he looked. "You want to hurt me to mark me as what? Is this how…is this what is meant by us becoming a couple?"

"Yes. No." After opening the door to the shower, he picked her up and sat her on the counter. "I'm going to dry you off. Then we'll dress. I need to explain this to you."

His cock was so hard that it looked painful. When she reached down and wrapped her fingers around him, she marveled that her fingers didn't touch. Moaning, he rocked into her hand and then pulled back. But Thor simply reached for him again, stepping off the counter and kneeling before him.

"I want to taste you now." He moaned, a growl really, but he didn't tell her no. "I've never done this before, so if I don't do it right, will you tell me?"

"If you don't want me to come in your mouth, now would be the time to tell me. Because as much as I'd like to do that, I'm not going to be able to stop once I start." The thought of him coming in her mouth made her moan. She looked up at him as she licked him from root to crown. "Christ love, you're going to kill me."

His cock was thick and long. She loved the way he felt both silky and hard, the way the skin on his cock moved with her tongue. And his taste was like nothing she'd ever experienced before. Lost in what she was doing, when Kaleb growled low and pulled her away from him, she whimpered.

"Finish me." His voice was hard, commanding, but it didn't frighten her. It made her wet that she'd made him so out of control. "Finish me now, Thor, before I turn."

She saw it then, the bear. He was rushing along Kaleb's skin until she had a hard time finding him from the bear. Taking him into her mouth again, he rocked hard, fucking her mouth as he'd done her pussy the night before. With the first taste of him, his essence, she slid her fingers into her and pinched her clit to try to find some relief. When he roared out his release, Thor had to work fast to swallow all of him. There was no way she was missing any of him.

Her body hurt. Not from what he'd done to her but because she'd been denied for so long. And when he jerked her up from the floor, pulling her along behind him to the bedroom, she had a moment of fear. Before she could tell him to stop, to take a breath, she was tossed onto the bed. Bouncing twice, she was pulled to the edge by him, and he entered her. A hard, quick punch of him entering her had her breath swoosh out of her.

"Christ, you're going to pay for that." His cock filled her to where she knew he was in the back of her throat. "You're going to be mine now. All mine."

"Yes." She wrapped her legs around him, her ankles locking of their own accord. Nuzzling his neck, she could smell him, his scent taking her so close to the pinnacle that she was begging him to give her what she needed. And when he bit her, sank sharp, sharper than human teeth into her throat, she screamed out her release, screamed out even as she sank her own teeth into him.

Blood filled her mouth, strong, spicy, and hot. Dizziness swamped her as she swallowed him down. He pounded into her body even as his blood poured down her throat. When she came again, darkness descended upon her and stars danced over her open eyes. She had to close them as something filled her mind.

Memories of him, small snippets of his life. The day he'd met Samuel. Then later when he'd met Stephen and a man named Hawk. The woman who'd given him life...not his mother, but she'd bet the witch, on the day she'd told him he'd find a mate and that she'd be his world. Thor had a moment of fear that he'd meet her someday and she'd be alone, but more days, weeks of his life filled her. When she cried out again, the pain of his changing to a bear filling her, Thor let the darkness take her under.

~~~

Samuel felt the connection. It was profound and had him stagger to his seat. It took him several moments of breathing deeply before he realized that it was a mating bond between Thor and Kaleb. And yet it was so much more.

He'd had a feeling for years now that Kaleb was more than he'd said. A werebear wasn't a species that Samuel had had a great deal of contact with, but he knew that while Kaleb had never said he was more than simply a shifter, he had hinted that he had powers that were great. And Samuel was pretty sure that Stephen knew it as well.

"Did you feel that?" Kennedy sat down as she waddled into the room. "I thought me to be in labor, but then I realized it wasn't coming from me. Did ye feel it?"

"Yes. It was Thor and Kaleb. I believe they've mated and bonded." He was feeling a good deal better and stood up to go to his wife. "How are you feeling, love? You're doing okay?"

Kennedy was due the previous day, but the doctor had told them that everything was fine. Samuel didn't want to alarm anyone, but he didn't think his wife was okay at all. She looked about ready to burst.

"Fine. I'm tired is all. This morning I went for a walk in the forest for a bit of air. Did you know there are several *póilíneachta* running around?" It took him a second to translate she'd meant police, but before he could tell her they were his men and were necessary, she continued. "Every time I moved, one of them was there to help me over a log or to offer to go and get ye're car for me. I can walk and be alone, you know."

"I'm sure they do as well, but I think they simply want to make sure you don't have this baby in the forest." He was terrified she'd have it somewhere there were no drugs...not for her, but for him. He wasn't going to make it. "Besides, I'm reasonably sure you told them you were fine."

"Aye, I did. Several times as a matter of fact." She stretched out her legs, and he got up to put them on his lap. "I've a question for you. Do you remember that man Vinnie told us about? The one who does the work on old furniture?"

"Yes. Russel Hawkmen. I think he goes by Hawk. Why? Do you have some old antiques that you didn't tell me about?" She smiled and nodded her head. "You thinking of having an affair with him?"

"Nay, I'm thinking we need to have some of the things from Ireland brought over for our daughter. *Seanmháthair* is coming here, and when she does, I'd like for her to make us a list." Samuel nodded, liking the idea. Kennedy's grandmother was a wonderful woman, and he loved her as much as his own mom. He thought about getting the five of them together. He'd like—

"Girl? I thought you said a son?" She grinned at him, and he tweaked her toe. "Not nice. I was afraid there for a minute. Especially when I think of how long it took us to decide on a paint color for his room."

"I didn't take that long. I said blue. You're the one who went to the store nineteen hundred times trying to find the perfect color." She rubbed her hand over her extended belly. "I've a mind to have Thor and Kaleb over for dinner tonight. Do ye think you can persuade Jimmy and Gab to come too?"

"Yes. And I'll invite Stephen, too, along with Vinnie if you don't mind. And if I can find him, Hawk. We'll make a night of it." She nodded and put her feet on the floor. "When are we going to the doctor?"

"This afternoon. I'm going to tell Butler that we're having guests for dinner. Something simple if you don't mind." He told her steaks on the grill was fine with him. Nodding, she left him to his work, and he moved to his desk. Samuel did have a lot to catch up on, and the sooner he got it finished, the more time he would have. He really didn't want to have to work when they were finished with the doctor.

Samuel was buried in a file when his phone rang. He nearly didn't answer it but picked it up with a bark of his name. The person at the other end was quiet for a few seconds before he finally spoke. Samuel didn't have time for this shit.

"I was wondering if you know of a Tania Thornton." Samuel stopped breathing for a second and nearly told the man to fuck off when he continued. "She's been missing for several weeks now and we're looking for her in connection with the deaths of three other officers."

"You don't say." Samuel reached for Kaleb and hit a wall. Either the man was sleeping or blocking him. Either way, he needed him. Picking up his cell phone, he dialed him while speaking to the man on the other end of his house phone. "Who is she? Or you for that matter?"

"Oh, I'm her boss. Captain Lyod Sweeney. Someone mentioned that she was staying at your clinic, and I wanted to confirm that." Samuel finally hung up his phone and reached for Stephen when Kaleb didn't answer. He nearly missed what Sweeney said. "Her fingerprints, you see, are coming up all over the crime scene."

"You do know it's in the middle of the afternoon, don't you? Whatever you want had better be —"

"I'm on the phone with Sweeney, and he knows that Thor was at the clinic. He's saying her prints are all over the crime scene. Not possible, I know, but I need you to see if they're all right. I can't contact Kaleb." To the man on the phone he answered as quickly as he could. "I don't know who you're talking about, but if you need information about the patients at the clinic, I'm afraid that the law states that I don't have to give you that. Even if I had it."

Stephen told him he'd go right now as Sweeney spoke. "It's not nice to lie to the police. I'm a very powerful man, and I can rain trouble down on your head so quickly and so hard you'll never see the light of day again. If you could have her call me, or better yet, come to the station house, I'd be very grateful."

"Threatening me will get you nothing but your own shit ton of trouble, buddy. And even if I knew where she was, there is no fucking way that I'd tell her shit about you. You fucking call here again and I will—" Samuel looked up when Butler came into the room and sliced his fingers across his throat. Samuel knew he wanted him to hang up and simply put the receiver in the cradle. "What is it?"

"The alarm, sir. It's beeping. It's saying that you're being traced. Though why they'd trace a call that they made is beyond me, but I wanted you to know." Samuel nodded and thanked his man. "I have heard from the missus that we're to have guests this evening. Might I assume that this will be more than a social call?"

"You can. Though for the record I'd very much like for it not to be at the table." Butler nodded and smiled. "Do you think maybe we can have a meal that will have us all moaning and groaning about how good it is and not think about all this shit?"

"I think that can be arranged. And my missus has had it in her head that we're to have an apple pie, sir. And we've unearthed the ice cream maker as well. Would that suit you?" Samuel told him it would. "Very good, sir. I'll see what I can put together for you tonight."

After Butler left, Samuel waited to hear from Stephen. No more than a few seconds later, Stephen, Kaleb, and Thor were standing in his office. Thor was not at all happy with any of them.

"I said we would drive over. This rolling through the air like a sonic jet is not...Christ, I'm going to be sick." When she took off running to the hallway, Kaleb followed her. Stephen sat in the chair across from his desk.

"She's pissed at me." Samuel laughed. "I think it's funny because she thinks she can yell at me and I'll be sorry. All I can think about is how her face looked when I showed up in the bathroom with her and Kaleb."

"You went into their bathroom? Are you nuts?" Stephen shrugged and smiled. "She is going to kill you. You know that right?"

"She might try, and I might let her hit me. But she won't kill me. She has my blood. Can't do it." Stephen leaned back in the chair. "I was feeding when you called me. I don't normally do that during the day, but she was there, and I was in the mood for—"

"Enough please." Stephen laughed again. "Sometimes too much information like that could get you into trouble. You know that right?"

They both stood up when the couple came back into the room. Butler was right behind them with a large tray with what smelled like pumpkin and tea. The scones on the plate still had steam coming off them, and Samuel felt his mouth water.

"I've taken the liberty of making a light repast. I'll have a luncheon ready in thirty minutes, as well as iced tea for those who would like it." Butler looked at Stephen as he continued. "Sir, your package has been delivered and has been stored per your instructions. Will you require some refreshments as well?"

"No thanks. And thank you for suggesting that I have it here." When Butler nodded and left the room, Samuel raised a brow at Stephen. "Blood. In the freezer. When I left here a couple of weeks ago, I was hungry, and that's when your good man suggested I have a storage here. I even put in a freezer in that massive pantry you have. You should have seen the look on his face when I asked him if I could store some of his blood there. I thought he'd have a kitten."

"Christ, I'll be lucky if he stays now. And good idea on the other. I'd really hate for you to get stuck here and not be able to get out for what you need. But you know that I'd never let you go hungry." Samuel had fed Stephen once when he'd been too hungry to leave the house. But there were more pressing things going on, and right now that was foremost in his mind. He turned to Kaleb.

"Sweeney called here a few minutes ago. And when I couldn't get in touch with you, I had Stephen make sure you were all right."

"He came into the bathroom with us." Samuel tried to hide his laughter at the look on Thor's face, but she knew. "You son of a bitch, you told him to come there?"

"Christ, no. I told him to find you and make sure you were all right. I never told him...he did that all on his own." Samuel had to take several deep breaths before he could continue. "But we do have a problem with Sweeney. He threatened me and mine. And that just doesn't fly with me."

"I'll take care of him." Samuel glanced at Kaleb when Thor spoke. The man was as relaxed as he'd ever seen him. "I'm the one to do it, and you know it."

"I'll help, but she is the better man for the job." Kaleb stood up and kissed Thor on the mouth before turning to him. "I've something to tell you. I should have long ago but I never wanted...I wasn't very happy with my life when I met you, and now that I have Thor...well, I think it's time."

"You're scaring him, Kaleb; just tell him." At that moment, Samuel knew that somehow Stephen was aware of what Kaleb had to tell him. And that was scarier than simply not knowing.

"I'm well over two thousand years old, and I've been touched by a witch's magic."

Chapter 7

Lyod watched the man in front of him. Who knew that someone as stupid as this man always appeared to be could fall into so much information in so little time? Lyod picked up the picture that he'd handed him when he came in three days ago. Lyod remembered the conversation he'd had with him that led to him calling Samuel Payne.

"You say you found her on this large estate this morning?" Danny Swindle had nodded and smiled. "I'm assuming you didn't let her or any of the others know what you were up to."

"Nah. I just snapped those with my phone and took them home to print up. I heard you were looking for her and so was the mayor." He'd laughed like he had not a care in the world. "You'd have had to be stupid not to see him begging everyone to tell him where she is. He's got a real hard on for her, don't he?"

"He does indeed." Lyod had picked up the picture again and looked at the crisp picture of Thornton, trying to erase the memory of the other day. He wondered what miracle drug she'd taken, because there was no way she looked this good after everything they'd done to her. He wondered if by now she was glowing. The fucking cunt always landed on her feet. Lyod tossed the picture on the desk again and glared at the man. He didn't want a picture of her. He wanted her dead.

"I called this man, the one that owns this estate. Did you know that he's a billionaire?" Danny shook his head. "He claims he doesn't know where she is. And from all accounts, she doesn't appear to be staying there now either. I don't suppose you have any idea where she is now, do you?"

"I don't know. That was the last time I went to look for you. You said to back off." Lyod wished now that he'd had the man stay on her. He'd been his only resource. "I can go back if you want me to. No hardship to me."

Lyod had to admit he was excited. To have her so close was enough to give him a chubby. But to Danny he only looked like he was thinking it over. Letting this guy find her and keep tabs on her would keep him under the radar, and the mayor out of the picture. Besides, Lyod had plans for the mayor, and in a few days the city would be looking for someone to replace him. Lyod wondered if he should apply for the job. Mayor Lyod Sweeney had a nice ring to it, he thought. But he looked at Danny, who was looking at him expectantly.

"You do that. Report only to me what you find and where she's staying. I want all you can find out about the people she's staying with, too. Off the record." Danny nodded and smiled. "You'll be on leave with pay until she's brought in. I don't want her to know that we have tabs on her."

"But the mayor? He'll know that I found her, right?" Lyod nodded. "Good. I sure could use that reward that he's posting. I can make a real good back payment on my house."

Good to know the man had debt. Lyod could always use that against one of his men when he got a little too out of hand. After Danny left, he picked up the picture and called Ansell. There was going to be hell to pay, he knew that, but for now, he had something to give him.

"So you decided to call, did you? Well, it was nearly too late." Lyod didn't care for the sound of that but hurriedly told him what he knew.

"We have a lead. I tried calling the guy out who has her, but he's not budging. I have someone watching the place now, so I should have something very soon." Ansell snorted, but Lyod continued before he could comment. "She was last seen with a man named Payne, Samuel Payne. He's reported to be worth billions and has a house that is nearly impossible to get into. I plan to pay him a little visit today."

"And this is helpful to me how? You promised me that she'd be dead by now. Swore to me that with the damage that was done to her not only would she not be able to tell anyone what happened to her, but her body was more than likely rotting in a place where no one would find her. And now not only is she alive and kicking, but she's living with a man who I know personally is more savvy at keeping others safe than anyone I fucking know." His voice had gotten progressively louder as he spoke, and by the time Ansell drew a breath, no doubt to continue, he was practically screaming at him. "Get this fucking bitch now, and if I hear one more excuse for why she's not dead, I'm going to show you how I deal with sons of bitches that fuck me."

"I'm working on it." Ansell started to speak again, but Lyod cut him off. "I'll have her to you by the end of the week. If not, I'll do whatever it is you think I deserve. I swear to you."

"You'd better fucking have her here by Friday or so help me, you'll never live to see Saturday." The phone slammed down, and Lyod felt the sweat pour down the back of his shirt, which frightened him because he was suddenly cold. Picking up the picture of Thornton and the other men, he wanted to tear it into shreds, hoping that she'd feel it. Knowing it was stupid, he got up to call for his car. It was time to pay her a visit.

The drive over to the house was long. Traffic was backed up because of idiots going to work and the added problem of road work. It seemed that no matter where you wanted to go in Ohio, there was no way to get there. Road construction seemed to be the number one way to spend money in this state. By the time he pulled up in front of the address, he had to check twice to make sure he had the right one. Mother fuck, this place was huge. But then he should have expected that. The man was worth more than even Ansell was.

"I'd like to speak to Mr. Samuel Payne, please," Lyod told the disembodied voice at the front gate. "I don't have an appointment, but it's important that I see him."

"May I ask who this is please?" The woman sounded like she had an accent but from where, Lyod couldn't tell. "And if you have no appointment, you may not be able to see him today."

"I'll take my chances." Lyod smiled smugly. Being a cop did have some perks. "Tell him it's Captain Lyod Sweeney of the Columbus Vice Squad."

The woman asked him to wait, and so he did. Taking out his phone, he called his office to tell them he'd be a little late and for his secretary to cancel all his morning meetings. By the time he'd answered three emails and taken another call from the mayor, he realized he'd been sitting there for nearly twenty minutes. As he reached for the intercom again, he saw a man standing near the closed gate. Getting out, Lyod started forward.

"Stay back." The venom in the man's voice startled him, and Lyod found himself stopping despite his desire to talk to the man. "What the fuck are you doing here? I thought I made it clear that I didn't want to speak to you."

"Mr. Payne?" The man moved even closer and Lyod, even with the gate between them, had a moment of terror. "I wanted to come and speak to you about Thornton. We might have gotten off on the wrong foot."

"Damned right we did. What the fuck do you want? And so you know, that fucking idiot you sent here to watch the house is no longer with us. I've had him killed and buried in a shallow grave in the back of your yard." Lyod took a step back and put his hand on his weapon. "Touch it and you'll die where you stand."

"I would listen to him if I were you. He's not at his best in the morning, and when you shit in his oatmeal, as you've apparently done, things are ten times over fucked up." Lyod turned to see the large man behind him. "I'm Jimmy, and if he gives me the okay, I'm going to rip your throat out and feast on you for a snack."

"I just wanted to talk to him about Thornton. I think—" The man now in front of him took one step closer, and that's all it took for Lyod's bladder to let go. Lyod would swear for the rest of his life that the man looked like a giant wolf for a few seconds. "I'd like to go now."

Jimmy nodded and crossed his arms over his chest.

"Are you going to allow me to leave here?"

"Depends." Lyod asked him on what. "Whether or not you can be gone before I count to ten. One...Two...."

Lyod ran to his car door and dropped his keys three times before he was able to get them in the door. By then the man was on number six and still counting. When his car was in reverse, he heard the man say ten and suddenly he was gone, and in his place was the biggest fucking wolf he'd ever seen. And he was pissed. Looking at the gate showed him not one but two lions who looked like they'd been fed super growth formula their entire life. Slamming his foot on the gas pedal, he raced down the street before he was killed. Mother fuck.

Lyod had to pull over about fifteen minutes later. He was shaking so hard he hurt, and he realized he was sobbing. He'd never been so terrified in his life. And there was no way he was going back to that house, even if Ansell held a gun to his head. Enough was enough. Picking up the phone with shaking hands, he had to put it down again, unable to press any buttons. Ten minutes after pulling over, he was back on the road again, having come to some major decisions.

"I'm done." He felt better hearing his own voice in the sedan. "I'm going to clean out my safe, take my money and anything else I can get my hands on before tonight, and I'm fucking out of here."

He had a great deal of ready money where he could get to it without hitting the bank. It would have been stupid of him to have put it all in any place where it could have been traced back to him. Lyod had taken precautions in the event of an emergency. He was pretty sure this was a first-class emergency. First things first, he had to get things squared away at home and take care that his ex-wife got nothing from the house. And if he was to return, he wanted to make sure that there wouldn't be a firing squad there waiting for him. His personal checking account was always nearly empty, just the way he thought it should be. He had all his cash in places all over the house and yard. He was set.

"Then when I have everything ready, I'm going to drop off this planet like I was never here, and never hear of Ansell or Thornton ever again." He wasn't sure it would be that easy, but he was willing to try. This place had gotten way too nuts.

When he pulled into his drive, he felt a good deal better. He'd thought of leaving and what he'd be leaving behind, and tried to think of another way to get Thornton to Ansell. While he was still scared shitless, he knew on some level that what he'd seen wasn't real. "Who changes into a wolf and a lion? No one. They might have drugged me or did one of those hypnosis things with my mind."

Not that he really believed that, but he was willing to believe anything over a man changing into a wolf. Moving to his bedroom, he stripped off his clothing and stepped into his shower. The sooner he got the stench off him the better he'd feel. An hour later, he was standing in the kitchen drinking a cup of coffee when his cell phone rang.

"There are three meetings for after lunch that I've tried to change. The one with the mayor is set, and he said if you're not there that he'll find someone who will be. What would you like to do about it?" Lyod told her he'd make it. "The meeting with your ex-wife's lawyer is mandatory. He said if you missed this one, he would drag this out for years by taking you to court every few weeks until she gets what she wants. And there is a meeting with a man by the name of Kaleb Jonas. I've looked him up. There is not a lot about him, but I was able to find that he's affluent and has been noted as something of a humanitarian. My sources say that he donated the money to have the library redone."

"Cancel the one with the lawyer. I've won this one, and she'll just have to get over it. As for Jonas, did he say what he wanted?"

"Just that he wanted to speak to you." What harm could it do really? Lyod told her to keep that one as well. "What time will you be in?"

"Soon. I have a couple of things to see to about a case. Then I'll be in. Should be there...." He looked at the clock on the wall, surprised to see it was only just after nine. "I'll be there by eleven. Hold down the fort until then."

After hanging up, he poured himself some fresh coffee and sat down at the computer in the kitchen. He was just pulling up information on Jonas when his cell phone rang. When he saw who it was, he ignored it. He wasn't in the mood to talk to his ex-wife right now.

By the time he'd started his journey to the office, he knew nothing more about Jonas. But he did have some information about the library project. The man had footed the entire bill of just over six million dollars. And no matter how many times he tried to find a picture of the man, he ran into blurred photos or ones with Jonas's hand in front of the camera. The man was a ghost.

Well, in a few hours he'd have his picture as well as a fingerprint. Lyod was going to find out about the man if he had to shoot him for DNA. Smiling, he entered the building and went straight to his office. Lyod was glad that he'd nearly forgotten about the wolf and lion.

~~~

"What do you mean you're going to go see Sweeney? Are you fucking nuts?" Kaleb sat down on the bed and watched Thor pace. She was in a fine snit, and he was having entirely too much fun watching her.

"I want to see what the man is worth. You yourself said you're not one hundred percent sure that he's in on this. I can find out for you." She snorted. "Why don't you come here and let me relax you again?"

Last night after they got back from Samuel's house, he'd taken her to bed. Christ, the woman may be a novice at making love, but she certainly made up for it with her willingness to learn. She might just kill him before too long. When she stopped moving and turned to look at him, he felt his cock thicken. His need for her rolled over him in strong waves as he watched her.

"You think you're going to distract me from what you're doing?" There was no sense in denying it, so he nodded. "I don't want to have sex with you again."

"Now that's a lie if I ever heard one. I can smell you." He stood up and pulled his shirt over his head. "Come here, love, and let me have you."

Her backing up made him smile. There was nowhere for her to go, and he wanted her.

"Leave me alone. I'm not finished with this."

"We'll take it up later if you want. Take off your shirt for me. I want to see you." She shook her head, and he reached out a hand to touch her breast. "Your nipples are hard, and your pretty pussy is wet for me."

"You can't solve everything with sex." He leaned into her throat slowly and kissed her pounding pulse. "Kaleb, I'm serious. You need to stop this so we can talk."

He pressed his body to hers, holding her against the wall. Lifting her hands up, he held them in his left hand while he cupped her ass with his right. She was flush against him now, and his cock ached to be inside of her.

KATHI S. BARTON

"Talking is overrated anyway. Besides, for as much as your lovely mouth is saying no, your body is begging me to take you." Pulling her up, he rocked into her. When she moaned, Kaleb nipped at her neck before looking down at her. "I really need to be inside of you."

When he let go of her hands, she put them on his shoulders and he lifted her up. Both her legs wrapped around his hips, and he fit himself in the cradle of her thighs. She moaned when he moved deeper into her.

"I hate that you can do this to me without any effort." He laughed at her statement, wondering if she realized how hard he worked at keeping from taking her every twenty minutes. "Do you have any idea how you make me feel when you do this?"

"I do. I feel the same." He put his hands down the back of her jeans and cupped her bare ass. "These have to go."

The sound of her pants tearing from her body made him hurt. Taking her mouth savagely, he stabbed his tongue into her mouth like he wanted to do with his cock. When she was gloriously naked from the waist down, he tore her shirt off her, too. Moving his mouth down her neck to her breast, he continued to fuck her through his jeans.

"Please, Kaleb, fill me." Panting, he looked down at her. Her need was right there where he could see it, almost taste it. Pressing her harder against the wall, he reached down to free his cock and moaned when she wrapped her hand around him. "I want to taste you again."

"I can't, love. If you take me into your mouth right now, I'm going to hurt you fucking you." Pulling her up enough that his cock was just to her entrance, he lowered her over him and slid into her wet heat. "Christ, you're hot. And tight."

When he was buried to his balls in her, he paused. His climax was so close that if he didn't, she'd be left high and dry. Nipping at her breast and suckling on her nipple, he reached between them with his free hand and found her hard clit.

"Do you have any idea what it does to me to have you wrapped around me like this?" He rocked his hips slowly and rolled himself harder against her. "It's like having everything good come to me, and knowing you're all mine makes it all the better."

Her breasts rubbed against his chest hairs, and he felt her tighten around him. Taking her ass into both his hands, he fucked her slow and easy. Watching her face while her own release moved to the edge and then over was the greatest thing he'd ever witnessed. And when his own climax took him, it felt as if he'd been given a gift. A great and wonderful gift. Kissing her as he filled her, Kaleb felt his heart open, and he fell in love, head-over-heels in love with his mate. There could be nothing better in the world than this, he thought.

Feeling her head on his shoulder as her body continued to spaz and tremor, Kaleb moved them both to the bed. Laying down with her still wrapped around him, he felt his cock jerk to life again. Moving slowly inside of her, he waited to see if she could take him again. When her legs tightened around his hips, he pulled her hands up to the head board.

"Don't touch me just yet." She curled her fingers into the iron work, and Kaleb ran his hands down her arms to her waist. "I want to mark you again, but this time I want to let my bear take you."

"You mean him have sex with me?" He might have laughed at her incredulous tone, but his bear perked up at that moment, and he had to calm him.

"No, I was just going to let a little of him go for now so he could bite you. But when you're changed, if you want to be, he's going to take you as many times as you'll let him." His bear snarled at him. "You've made him very needy."

"Tell him to behave." Her body bowed up off the bed when he moved down her with his mouth. "Is this him or you? Because I have to tell you, this is fucking fantastic."

"It's me and him." Kaleb let his bear go enough that she could see him along his face. "He wants to taste you."

Thor opened her thighs, and he sat up. Kaleb felt like he was being torn in half. His beast wanted him to let go so he could take her, and Kaleb wanted to bury himself deep inside of her again and again. Leaning down to her apex, Kaleb buried his nose deep into her.

"Kaleb." He chuckled when she screamed, and he entered her with his tongue. He knew it was going to be different for her; his bear's tongue was longer and a good deal thicker than his. When she screamed again, this time flooding his mouth with her cream, Kaleb drank greedily from her as they both, he and his bear, took their fill.

When she came a third, then a fourth time, riding his mouth as she did, he pressed his finger into her pussy and licked a path along her thigh. When she came the next time, he let go enough that his bear could mark her. Her scream let him know that she was hurt, but she came again as he bit her more deeply.

"Change me." He started to look up at her to see if he'd heard her correctly. "Now, do it now. Change me into you so I can run with you."

"I have to hurt you more than I am now." She moaned when he tore at her flesh. "Baby, I don't know if I can do this. I don't want to hurt you."

She jerked her leg, tearing open her vein there. Lapping quickly at the blood as it flooded his mouth, Kaleb felt his bear take more of him. There was no way he could save her as a human. Her only chance of survival was for her to be taken. Letting his beast go, he felt his nails dig deeply into the mattress as he held on. Christ, he never meant for this to happen.

Chapter 8

When she opened her eyes, she had to shut them again. Thor peeked beneath her lids and saw that she'd seen correctly. There was a small person on her chest. Before she could swat it away, someone spoke to her left.

"She wanted to see your face up close. Don't ask me why they do that, but they're harmless enough and they do make life interesting." Thor looked at the woman curled into the chair next to the bed. "Hi. I'm Gab Burger. You and I met the other night at Samuel's house. And my husband is Jimmy, Jimmy Burger."

"I remember...hi." The little person moved when Thor sat up. "Do you know what this is? And how I get her to stop staring at me like this?"

"She's a pixie. And no, you'll find out that once they know you're awake, they'll all be in here. But you don't have to worry, they aren't allowed to change the bedrooms." Gab stood up, and Thor noticed that she was very pregnant. But instead of looking like a bloated cow like some women she knew did, she looked like a goddess. "Thanks."

It took Thor a few seconds to realize Gab had read her mind. "I guess I should have known that. I mean why not? You have a pixie in the house."

The door opened, and a man carrying a large tray walked in. As soon as he cleared the door, the room seemed to come alive with sparkly wings. There must have been over five hundred of the little suckers flying all over the room. Thor turned to Gab.

"If you just let them hang out a little while, they'll leave you alone." The tray was put across her lap as Gab continued. "They're part of this house they built. Jimmy and I are sort of used to them, but there are times when I'd just as soon they moved out. But they do have their uses."

Taking a look at the food in front of her, she looked at Gab. "Who the hell was he thinking to feed with all this?"

There were two thick roast beef sandwiches and a salad twice the size of any she'd seen in a family-style restaurant, as well as a bowl of buttered potatoes, a pile of green beans, and half an apple pie. Along with three bottles of water, there was a carafe of what smelled like coffee, and another of what looked like juice. All in all, there was enough food for a half dozen people.

"You'll be surprised at how hungry you are now and how much you can pack on. The best part is you never gain an ounce." Gab moved to the door as she finished. "I know you're a bit overwhelmed because of the pixies, but I'm to assure you that Kaleb is fine."

"He brought me here." She nodded. "Why? And where the fuck is he?"

Gab laughed. "I knew you'd get around to it. But he's at a meeting with the others. It seems that you were right in your assumption that Sweeney had something to do with your being hurt. He and the others, most I think you know, are working to get a better security system put in at your home. And just so you know, yours and Kaleb's home, not the little one you lived in before."

"And why is he assuming that I'm going to be living in his house?" Gab laughed again, this time sending the pixies up in the air for a moment. "Why are there so many of these things here anyway?"

"They helped Vinnie build the house to protect me. And they're not all pixies. Most of them are faeries, as well as a few brownies." She seemed so serious that Thor hesitated before laughing. "You should see the ones that didn't want to come in here to bother you."

With that, she moved out of the room, closing the door behind her. Thor looked around at the dozen or so people, or whatever they were called, that were left behind. One of them landed on her tray and sat on her roll. It was everything she could do not to pinch herself.

"You should know that we love Kaleb. He's been our champion for as many years as we can count." She smiled at Thor and then stood to bow before her. "I am Ana, a faerie. You're the Lady Jonas."

"I'm just Thor." There was giggling to her right, and she looked at the person flying there. "Do you think you could, I don't know, sit somewhere? And what do I call you? People? Faerie? Figments of my imagination?"

"We're all faerie, but you can call us by name." Ana pointed to the girl that was just settling on the pillow next to her. "She's Calina. And she is a brownie. We're to serve you."

"Serve me? How does that work when I could smash you without thinking about it?" Calina squeaked, and Thor felt bad. "I'm sorry. I feel...well, I feel really weird. I wish Kaleb was here."

"We can assist you in many ways. There are many of us, and we can do much more than move furniture. Though that has been a delight, we have come to realize that we may be helpful in other ways. Such as the Lady Gab. She will birth her babe here and we will help her." Thor wasn't sure how that was supposed to work when she was reasonably sure that the kid would weigh more than them even at birth. But Ana continued as if she'd heard her thoughts. "We'll take her pain away, not assist with the birth. You are very literal, are you not?"

"I am. Especially when I'm stressed. There are a thousand thoughts going through my head right now, and it hurts." Calina moved to her and touched her head. The pain was immediately gone. "Thanks. How did you do that?"

"We are to assist you. And it is a pleasure for me to take away your pain." Thor leaned back against the pillow. There were more faeries in the room than she'd first thought, maybe five or six dozen of them. And they were all staring at her.

"Okay, let's get this thing worked out." She shifted on the bed. "First, I guess I'd like to get a shower and get dressed. If we're going to have a conversation, I'd rather not be naked." One of them giggled, and she pulled the sheet around her as she stood. As soon as her feet were under her, she started to pitch forward. Tiny hands held her upright or she might have fallen on her face. "Thank you."

"It is the shift that has weakened you. Perhaps you should eat something first." Nodding, Thor sat back down and picked up the sandwich. It was nearly to her mouth when she realized what Ana had said.

"Shift?" Several of the faeries that had joined Ana and Calina nodded with them. "As in it worked? I'm a bear?"

"Well, right now you are human." Ana looked at Calina. "Well, she is. Does she not know the difference?"

"I believe she was speaking that she can shift into one. Now who is being literal?" Ana tisked as she landed on her hand. "You are now a shifter, as is his lordship. You will need to await him to shift, however, as we are not equipped to help you with that. Do you understand?"

"It worked." Ana nodded and smiled. "I'm a bear, and I can shift into one whenever I want. This is amazing."

"It is." Ana smiled and told her to eat. "In the coming weeks you will need the extra food until your body adjusts to its new self. His lordship said that many times a female will be fertile when she first becomes her other. But sadly you are not."

Thor ate the sandwich while she thought about being pregnant with Kaleb's child. There wasn't any way for her to raise a child on her own, and as soon as this thing with her boss was finished, she had to move on. Yeah, she thought, she was a bear now, but that didn't mean that the two of them would ever make it.

As she finished off the half a pie without any problems, she leaned back and looked around the room. Everyone but she and Ana were gone. She started to ask her about it when she felt someone touching her mind.

"I was wondering if you'd ever wake." Kaleb. Ana must have known because she flew off the side of her tray where she'd been sitting and under the closed door. *"How are you feeling?"*

"Like I've been abandoned." Flushing, she realized how clingy she sounded and told him she'd just had the biggest meal in her life. *"I didn't think I'd ever eat all that."*

"You'll notice that you're going to be really hungry for the next few weeks. Eat when you feel the need. You won't get heavier, but your body needs the extra bulk. Not that you're heavy now...I think you could stand to put on a few more pounds."

"Like that's going to happen." She reached for her clothes that she'd just noticed at the foot of the bed. "Why am I here and not at your house? Or mine for that matter?"

"Your house is at my house now." Trying hard not to bristle at his tone, she waited for him to continue. "And your other house is being watched. I've had Vinnie and Stephen and a few of the faeries go in and get what they could find. But the furniture will have to wait. There's a car there as well as a big Harley that Vinnie wants to ride someday."

"The bike is in the middle of being rebuilt and isn't running. The car? I don't have a car." She tried to think about who would be parking in her garage when she thought of her father. "What kind of car is it?" Closing her eyes, she just knew he was going to tell her it was a piece of shit something and didn't have any plates. Fuck.

"POS Pontiac. I think it's older than you." Her father always drove pieces of shit since he couldn't afford anything better that someone else wasn't paying for, unless he'd stolen it. "If it's not yours, then whose is it, if you don't mind me asking?"

"My father's. He's more than likely moved in when I didn't tell him he couldn't. Fuck." She turned on the water and stepped under the spray as soon as it was hot enough. Washing her hair with quick strokes, she scrubbed her body with the big sponge she'd opened that still had the wrapper on it and the bottle of vanilla-scented soap that also had never been used. "I don't suppose you could have one of those guys transport me there or whatever they call what they do. I need to kick his ass out."

"*Yeah, Samuel told me what a bastard he is. I can take you there, but we'll have to wait until later. The house is nearly finished, but we might have a few guests for a while. I would count on forever.*" She asked him if they were faerie. "*I see you've met them then. Ana has been with me for centuries, and Calina is her cousin. And yes, we'll have them living with us much the same as Jimmy and Gab have them. I think we would do good to have them stay with you for a while. At least until we can get this thing with Sweeney figured out.*"

"*I can take care of Sweeney on my own.*" Thor jerked on her clothes after drying. "*I'm not completely stupid, you know. I can handle one fucking prick.*"

Kaleb was very quiet for a long time, and she knew she'd pissed him off. His emotions were tied with hers so tightly that she was having a hard time figuring out whose were whose. When he spoke, she knew that he was trying his best not to be pissy with her and to hold onto his temper.

"*I never thought you were stupid. In fact, I would say you're the smartest person I know. Most of the time. But how long do you think you'll be able to hold onto your sow if he pisses you off? Not long at all, I would imagine, and a sow can be pissy when she's upset. And once you're a bear, a pissed off one, how soon after you tear him to shreds do you think it'll take the local cops to find you? Ten, maybe fifteen minutes? Then what?*" Thor felt tears fill her eyes. This was an emotion she wasn't familiar with, feeling inadequate and foolish. Not that she didn't make mistakes...she made thousands of them daily, but in this she was ignorant, and she hated that. But he was not yelling at her like she'd done to him. And for some reason, it made her feel twice as stupid.

"*I'm sorry.*" He didn't say anything, but she could feel something float over her, something she would swear was love. "*And my father would piss me off. He's good at that. And he'll rob me blind if I don't go in there and see to this. I have guns there. They're in a safe, but I don't trust him not to try and get into it. I'm not worried about the money. I never had much of it there anyway, but the guns he'd sell to some kid, and then I'd feel responsible for their death."*

"All right. I'll come there to get you now." He didn't sound any less pissed at her, and she felt badly about that. *"I'm not your enemy, Thor. I'm your mate. And when you hurt, I hurt. When you're pissed off, I'm pissed off. But I have control over my bear; you do not."*

"I'm sorry." She made her way down the stairs. Ana was there at the bottom waiting for her. *"Ana is with me now. When you get here, will she stay here?"*

"No, she belongs to you. It's her choice, not mine. But she said that she would be honored to serve you, and she and Calina will be with you always." She felt his laughter. *"I would say that you're stuck with them, but I'm thinking that once you get to know them, you'll be glad for them. Ana is the straight one to Calina's goofy one."*

She wasn't sure if she could handle that, but said nothing. Thor would have to learn to curb her thoughts if this thing was going to last for very long. Following the faerie into what happened to be a kitchen, she met with a big man, Milford, the butler to the Burgers, and he was making her a light snack. Kaleb told her he was on his way.

~~~

Roger Thornton moved into the kitchen to look for something that might have the combination on it. Why the hell she had something this big in her house could only mean one thing: it had a lot of priceless shit in it. The man standing in the kitchen scared him enough that he cried out. When the man laughed, Roger felt his temper spit out.

"What the fuck are you doing in my house?" The man laughed harder. "You get out now before I call the police. They won't take kindly to you breaking and entering. I know how that one works."

"You do that. Call the cops. And last I heard, this wasn't your house." The man moved toward him in a slow gait that had Roger thinking he could take him. But when he was up close and personal, as his daughter used to say to him when he was going to hit her again, he took a step back. This guy was way bigger than anyone he'd had to tangle with.

"You should know that I'm watching this here house for my little girl. And she's not going to take too kindly to you coming in here like you own the place." Someone snorted behind him, and he turned to see his daughter, or spawn as he liked to call her when she wasn't around. "Tania? Whatcha doing here?"

"I live here, you fucking moron. What are you doing here?" She'd never had any respect for him, and he took a step toward her to show her some of his fist. But before he could get his hand into a fist to hit her, it was captured. The man behind him held him so tightly that Roger knew he was gonna break a bone or two.

"You're supposed to be in prison for another five years. What the hell are you doing out running free like real people? I think you should have gotten the chair, but they wouldn't let me be on the jury." Roger wanted to slap her face, but the man behind him hadn't let him go yet. "Well? And when you're finished telling that lie, tell me how you found me."

"I was released early for good behavior." She laughed, a sharp barking sound that set his teeth on edge. "You never did believe anything I said to you. You're my

111

spawn. Don't you know that you're to believe in me no matter what? That was your problem, Tania, you have no heart. None at all. And what little sense you have, you done used it up on God knows what sort of drugs. Drugs you never would share with your dear old dad, I'm betting."

"I don't do drugs. And if I had, you're right, I wouldn't have given them to you. But you're a liar and always have been. And as for being your spawn, I quit calling you my father long before I realized what a prick you really were. Long before you put Mom in an early grave. So again I ask you, what the fuck are you doing in my house?"

He eyed the man who'd finally let go of his hand, and wondered if he could get a quick punch in her face before he caught him again. He knew men like him. Roger knew he'd let him go when his spawn started bawling. Before he could make do on his plan, the man laughed and spoke.

"You're thinking that you can hit her and I'll only hold you down for a bit and then let you go." Roger nodded before he could think to do otherwise. "But I got news for you. You touch her, even to shake her hand, and I will rip your throat out and then piss on your head. Then I'll let her hurt you."

"Hurt me? You think I'm gonna survive you taking out my throat?" Roger tried to puff himself up bigger than his five feet, ten inches. But the man had at least eight inches on him. And he more than likely weighed about two hundred pounds more. "I think you should get yourself on out of here and let me and my spaw...Tania take care of this. Father and daughter like. You're just messing things up for me."

"Nope. You'll have to conduct your business with me here. And this way I can keep an eye on you." The man hopped up and was sitting on the counter like he owned the place. Roger decided to ignore him for now and turned to his daughter. She didn't look like she had when he'd been sent away. She seemed...well, fuller came to mind, but he knew that wasn't right.

"I'm going to call the police if you don't tell me what you're doing here." He started to lie to her but felt the overwhelming need to tell her the truth. He hated telling the truth when a lie would serve him so much better.

"I was told you had a house out this way. And when I found this'en, I knew it was yours. Then when I found your mail in the box, I knew it was the right place. Why didn't you tell me you'd run into some money? I would have helped you invest it right." She only crossed her arms over her chest just like her momma used to do. "I'm thinking you need to be taken down a peg or two. And I'm just the man to do it if you don't act like you're my daughter."

"You can think that all you want, but you come near me and whatever Kaleb had in mind for you will be nothing compared to what I'll do to you. I'm not ten anymore." She wasn't at that. Roger took a long look at the spawn he'd helped create. It looked like her mother was standing there looking all defiant. He found he wanted to teach her a lesson, but was suddenly afraid of who would be learning from whom.

"You got any money you can spot me?" She shook her head. "What about that big safe up there? You got something in there? If not, what's the sense in having it? Get on up there and open it and give me a quarter...no half of what's in there, and I'll go away for good."

He didn't think she believed that any more than she ever seemed to believe him. Instead of calling his bluff, she looked at the man still sitting in the counter. When she moved away to go to the stairs, Roger sat down. This was way easier than he thought it would be.

"How the hell did someone as much of a prick as you have a child like her?" Roger smiled. The man wasn't as dense as he'd first thought. "Oh, I don't mean to say that she's bad in any way, but you are. What I'm saying is she's a wonderful, caring person, and you are not. Her mother must have been a saint to have stayed with you long enough to conceive her."

"Now see here. You can't talk to me like that. I'm a man twice your age." Roger backed up when Kaleb hopped off the counter. For a second he'd been impressed. Roger knew that he'd be hurting for a month if he'd done that. "You should have more respect for your elders."

The sound of a gun sliding home had him stop moving toward the younger man. Not that he knew what he was going to do when he was there, but his temper always got him into trouble. Roger swallowed hard. He'd know that sound anywhere. It was a hand gun, Glock he would say, and whoever was behind him was getting ready to shoot. When something cold and hard touched him right behind his left ear, Roger felt his heart skip a beat.

"You're a piece of shit." He started to turn toward his spawn, but she jabbed him harder in the head with what he could now tell was truly the gun. "You're going to get yourself killed one of these days, and I hope to Christ it's me that does it."

"Now daughter. You should know that when you lower that gun I'm going to fucking beat you senseless.

Then I'm going to take that gun from you and shoot you in the fucking head. I've had enough of your shit today. Give me the fucking money now." He felt his temper rise when she jabbed him again. "Stop that right fucking now. Or so help me I'm going to—" Roger suddenly realized what the hell he was doing.

"To what? Come on, tell me what you plan to do to me when I have a gun to your fucking empty head." Kaleb leaned against the counter and said nothing. The man wasn't going to help him out, Roger realized. Not even man to man.

As Roger was pushed toward the back door, he had a thought to turn around and hit her. But he was more afraid of her than he wanted to admit, even to himself. When she shoved him out the door and he landed in the grass, he turned to glare at her. But again the gun pointed at him had him snapping his mouth closed.

"You come back here and I will shoot you. Not warn you. I won't give you any sort of head start either. I will blow your fucking tiny little brain out of that head of yours and dance in the little brain that splatters all over the ground. Do I make myself very clear?" Roger nodded and stood up, brushing the dirt off his clothes. "And if I hear one thing, one tiny little peep out of anyone that you're hanging around them or trying to borrow money you have no intentions of paying back, I will arrest you."

It took him three seconds for that to sink in. "You're a fucking cop? Mother fuckballs. Why didn't you say something in the first place? Mother…damn it all to hell. You are not my daughter any more. I'm quitting you. What the fuck are you doing being a cop anyway?"

As he stormed off, Roger felt good. He'd disowned her. A cop? A fucking cop? No child of his was going to be hanging with him and be a part of the worst parts of his life. Roger vowed that so long as he breathed, his daughter could go to hell. He was a childless man. That was until he needed something from her again. Or he found that she'd left the house and he'd get back in. He knew now that the safe held guns, and guns on the market sold for a lot of money. Money that he'd keep for himself.

"I'm not even going to mention her in my will." Laughing, he walked all the way down the street before he realized he'd forgotten the car. "Stolen anyway. Let her explain that one to her cop friends."

Roger pulled the money he'd found in her house and counted it out. Fifty-two dollars wasn't a lot, but he figured it would buy him a drink or two. Entering the first bar he came to, Roger was whistling a tune. Yeah, he thought, he was a free man.

Chapter 9

The stakeout was perfect. Lyod had all the right men in place, and all the players were in the house. Now all they had to do was wait on someone to do what he wanted. If not, he was ready for that as well. The plane ticket he'd purchased earlier that day was tucked neatly in his bag, and the car he'd purchased a while ago under an assumed name was gassed up and ready as well. But that wasn't going to be necessary. Thornton would be his before too much longer.

"What the hell is that doing here?" Lyod looked up as a large medic ambulance pulled in the drive as soon as the gate was opened. "You think she's killed them all?"

He'd told these men that Tania Thornton had left the department and had gone on a killing spree. Lyod had dug up all the unsolved cases that he could find and made everyone think that they were recent murders. Really he thought it was much too easy, and was sort of disappointed that it had been. He'd wanted someone to challenge him, and all of the men he'd picked for this job simply thought what he said was true.

"I doubt she'd kill the hand that feeds her." He glanced up at the house they were watching. Kaleb Jonas had a house that his would fit in three times over. And that didn't count the servants' houses and the pool house. "She's got herself a pretty good set-up here. I'm thinking it might be for something else."

He'd also found out that Payne had a crippled mother. Perhaps that was why they were there. The sound of the siren was fading as he stood up and walked to the gate. A large man was standing in the gate house and appeared to be sleeping, but for some reason Lyod thought the man as alert as he was.

"You think we should offer our assistance?" Lyod shook his head at one of the men, Marcum Donaldson, who'd been questioning his every move since they'd gotten there. "I think this is one of the dumbest plans I've heard of."

"So you've said. Several times now. We're sticking with this one until you come up with something better." And for all his bitching and moaning about Lyod's plan, the man had offered no other way of doing this. "Keep an eye on the gate. When it opens, we're to stop whatever drives out and see if our girl is in there."

Several "yes, sirs" had him feeling in charge, but Marcum still bitched. "If I had known we were going to be hiding out for hours, I would have brought my computer. At least then I'd have something to do with my time."

When the gates slid open forty minutes later, he moved to step in front of any vehicle coming out. It just happened to be the ambulance. And with their lights and sirens on, he knew he'd be hard pressed to not only make it stop, but he'd never be able to search it either. HIPPA was driving him insane.

The Health Insurance Portability and Accountability Act allowed no room for him to get the sort of information he used to get. Its ruling stated that reasonable efforts must be made to make sure the information on all documents was kept private, and if anyone so much as hinted at any of the information, hell would be paid. Doctors and nurses alike kept any and all information to themselves, and no amount of bribes could loosen their tongues. But the worst place he'd run into problems was the clinic that Payne owned. They couldn't be bribed, couldn't be threatened, and no one in the place would tell him a damned thing no matter how many times he went to the place to find out. They were as tightlipped as his ex-wife's legs were open to every Tom, Dick, and Harry who had a dick. And some that didn't.

And just as he figured, it didn't even slow down when he stepped in front of it and screamed out of the driveway. He did manage to stop the second car coming out, but as soon as the man driving got out of his car and started for him, Lyod had a moment of clarity. He was a dead man. It was that man Jimmy from the other day.

"Are you stupid or do you want me to snap your neck?" Lyod reached for his gun and found himself suddenly pressed against the hood of the car he'd stopped. His gun skittered across the pavement. "You think you're going to pull a gun on me, you motherfucker? I'll own your ass."

"I just want to talk to Thornton." Jimmy popped his head on the hood of the car as soon as the words left his mouth. Lyod decided that even if they handed Thornton to him on a silver platter, right now he thought maybe he'd decline. Finding her was beginning to be more trouble than it was worth. Then he remembered his men.

"They're not coming to help you." Lyod started to sit up but was slammed back down on the hood as Thornton continued. He wondered when the hell she showed up. "You're the stupidest man I've ever had the unpleasantness to know. Do you have any idea whose property you're fucking around on?"

"You're under arrest for murder." He heard her laugh and then he was suddenly standing up, facing her. "I can take you in myself so that nothing happens to you."

A large man came to stand behind her, and it wasn't until he put his hand on her shoulder that Lyod knew who he was. Kaleb Jonas was with her, and wasn't going to take this well. Lyod thought of the meeting he'd had with the man several days ago, and how he'd been afraid of Kaleb then as he was right now.

"I want you to leave Thor alone," he'd said to him. "Or else I'll make you regret it for the rest of your days. And so you know, that's not going to be very long."

"Are you threatening me?" Incredulously, the man had nodded at him and grinned. "There are laws against that. Are you aware of that?"

"There are also ones that say you aren't supposed to kill anyone, that you shouldn't sell drugs on school property, as well as prostitution. But here you sit, guilty of all three and a few more." He'd stood up then and seemed to grow in size, which had made Lyod press back in his chair because the man was already fucking huge. "Come near her again and I will kill you."

And now here he was. "You don't listen well, do you?" Lyod started to speak but was cut off by Thornton.

"You're going to get into your car and go away from here." He took a step toward her, and Jonas picked him up by his neck and held him there. Lyod hadn't even seen him move. Thornton continued. "You're the stupidest man I know. Leave here now and I'll pretend that I don't want to let him kill you. Come back, speak to me or anyone I know, and no one will ever find your body. Not that I think anyone would care if you're dead or not."

"You'll pay." Lyod found himself suddenly on the ground gasping for breath. He looked up at the two of them before speaking. "You two cannot get away with this. Manhandling an officer of the law, lying to the police, and pretending to be dead."

"I wouldn't have had to pretend anything if you and Lipscomb hadn't tried to kill me." He looked at her, shocked. She'd figured out he was there, too. "Oh yeah, I know you were helping him. Especially when all those men seemed to pour out of the house right when I was telling you I was there. Must have twisted up your panties tight around your balls knowing that I was about to stumble onto your little money maker. And you might want to check out your little stash, too. Ill-gotten gains are against the law, in the event you didn't know that."

"You stole from me?" He started toward her again, only to be brought up short by Jimmy. He'd forgotten all about the man. "She can't get away with this. How would you like it if she took all your money you worked hard to get?"

Jimmy simply shook his head. Didn't these people understand that he'd had to do all sorts of things to earn what he had? And not only that, but the things he'd done simply to ensure that no one knew about it. Sometimes he thought being a bad guy was harder than being a good one. But it paid a great deal more, and he'd come to realize that he really liked having money and the things that went with it.

"You're going to come with me now and we'll get this all sorted out." She laughed at him, and Lyod glared. "Do you have any idea what Lipscomb is going to do to me if you don't come along with me now? I have to give you up to him by Friday or he's going to be really pissed off. Just come with me and we'll explain what's going on."

"Yeah, like that's going to happen. Why don't I drive you there myself and we can get some lunch on the way?" Lyod nodded, thinking she'd finally give him what he wanted. "You fucking moron, you don't possibly think that I'd turn myself over to a murderer, do you? If you do, you're dumber than I thought."

"Don't be dense. He's not a murderer. Ansell has other people do that for him." Lyod was going to have to make her see reason. "Just come with me. How bad can it be?"

"You'd take me to him, wouldn't you? You'd turn me over to him so that what? He doesn't kill you first?" He told her that was the plan. "Incredible. Simply incredible."

When she turned her back to him and wrapped herself around Kaleb, it occurred to him that she was his lover. Probably sucking him dry, too. But when Jimmy stood in front of him, Lyod took a step back. Pain suddenly radiated from his entire face and darkness took him. He knew that he'd been hit, but never had a punch to the face made him drop like this. Before he blacked out completely, he heard her laughter. It was bitter and full of hate, and Lyod knew he was going to die.

~~~

Kaleb watched Thor. She hadn't said a word since they'd gotten back in the car. Jimmy glanced at him several times in the rearview mirror, but he didn't say anything. Both of them knew that she was hurting.

"Ansell Lipscomb was on my list to find and bring in. When I first started out on this hunt, it was simply to find a man who was known to be dealing drugs too close to the high school. But the deeper I dug, the more I found out." Neither he nor Jimmy spoke as Thor continued. "The night I went to his estate, I was alone. Not that it mattered to me if I was or not. Even when I had a partner I tended to do things on my own. But this should have been a two-man operation. The place was crawling with armed men."

"Where is the place?" Kaleb looked at Jimmy when he asked. "Once a cop, always a cop. Where did you find his place, honey?"

"Mulberry Court. Although I don't understand the Court part, because his place was the only one there. I found that he'd bought the entire subdivision. I guess to keep things the way he wanted them." Again he looked at Jimmy. Mulberry Court was only two streets over from where they'd found her that night. "I'd killed nine by the time I got to the house. And had taken out three dogs. I don't kill animals normally, but it was me or them. And I hadn't thought to bring a dart gun. When I contacted Sweeney, he told me to stand down. To wait. I thought then that it was odd of him to say that to me, but he'd been on me about this case since I brought it to his attention."

"But you couldn't let it go." She shook her head as she laid her head on his lap. Running his fingers in her hair, he watched her closely. Thor was not just hurting. She was devastated with this.

"They caught me almost as soon as Sweeney told me to back off. But the men coming out of the house were too much for me to do anything by that point but to fight or be killed. When I was hit from behind, I thought for sure I was dead, but I woke up in a cell. Ansell showed up after they'd beaten me to shit and let the men there with me take turns making me suffer. They had one minute to make me scream or he'd make them pay a fine. One dollar. That was the fine. One fucking dollar."

"How long did you last?" Kaleb knew her well enough to know that she'd have held out for as long as she could, but he'd seen what they'd done to her, and she wouldn't have been able to last forever. The knife wounds alone would have brought down a larger man than him.

"I don't know. But it was too long for some of them. After a while, the pain was so intense that I wasn't really feeling it. That's when they started to strip my flesh off." She rolled over and looked up at him as she continued talking. "Was it the blood from Stephen or you that healed me to the point where nothing is visible?"

"Mostly mine, but Stephen made it so you'd survive long enough for me to heal you. He knew when I'd come into the cell with you that you were my mate. I didn't tell him, but he knew. Before he left with you, he asked me what I was going to do." Kaleb looked out the window as they drove toward the hospital where Samuel and Kennedy were having a baby. "I told him that I wasn't going to take you, claim you. I said it was too late. I'd been too long on my own."

"Yet you did. Why?" He looked down at her and smiled sadly. "You still don't want me, do you?"

"Yes. With all my heart. Not only have I fallen in love with you, but I've found that I can no longer live without you. In fact, I'm not sure how I survived this long without you in my life. I know it's a cliché, but you do complete me." She put her hand on his cheek, and he kissed it. "I'm in love with you, Tania Thornton. Will you marry me?"

He hadn't meant to ask her then. Hell, if he was honest with himself, he'd never even considered asking her at all. But now that he had, he held his breath waiting for her to answer him, to say something that would give him an indication that she would be his wife.

"I'm not a great prize." He laughed. "I'm serious. I'm messy when I'm working. I forget to eat sometimes. I shower when I think about it, but most of the time I just change my shirt and get back to work. There are times when I will snap at you for no reason, then find a corner to cry in until I can come and tell you I'm sorry. Then I've got this—"

He pressed his hand gently over her mouth and smiled at her. "Is that a yes? Because none of that matters to me. When you forget to eat, I'll make you something and bring it to you. I have a staff to clean up after us, so that's not really a hardship. In fact I think they'd love to have someone to clean up after. I'm seldom home anymore, and they're bored, frankly. I'll scrub your back when you need a shower, and the rest? We'll figure it out as we go."

"Do I get a ring?" Laughing, he told her he'd buy her whatever she wanted. "I don't want a diamond. I like them and all, but they're too flashy. I'm not a flashy sort of woman."

"No, you're not. You're more of a...opals to match the creaminess of your skin, emeralds to go with the temper I've seen you have, and sapphires to compete with the fire in your eyes when I make love to you...kind of woman." Jimmy cleared his throat, and Kaleb looked up at him. "You have to get your own ring. I'm taken."

"We're at the hospital. And so you know, I'm stealing the line about the gems and stuff. Gab will eat that up. And with her hormones all over the place right now, she might let me hold her without bursting into tears."

Kaleb waited until his friend got out of the car before he spoke again. Looking down at his one and only true love, he fell deeper in love with her. "I have to tell you what else you're going to be able to do now that we're mated. The witch that I helped that day gave me so much power that you're going to be someone to contend with." She nodded and sat up. "Did you ever tell me yes?"

"Yes. I'll marry you. But there are conditions." Before she could start on her no doubt long list, he pulled her to him and kissed her. Just touching her, having her skin so close to his, had his cock thicken to be deep inside of her.

"When we're finished here, I'm going to take you back to our home and take you to the woods. There are so many ways I want to make love to you, and my beast wants his share of your sow." Her moan made him growl. "You're going to love being fucked as my bear."

"You've called me that before. A sow...what is that?" He pulled her into his lap to kiss her. But she pulled back to make him answer her.

"A female bear. I'm a boar. And any children we have will be called a sow, too, or a cub. And though we normally do not run in groups, a group of bears is called a sloth." He rocked his hips upward and into her soft folds. "I want you right now."

Nodding, she laid back, and he took her to the seat. He tried to be careful of her clothing, but his need was too much. Buttons flew all over the back seat and floorboard as he tore at her shirt. When her breasts were naked, he took one into his mouth and suckled hard.

His shirt came up his back, and he sat up just long enough for her to pull it the rest of the way off. Taking her mouth again, he worked his hand down the back of her pants and pulled her bared ass up so he could rock into her again and again. Finally, he had to sit up and pull her pants off. But before he could taste her, like he really needed to do, she was tearing his pants open. Reaching for her to take her, he threw back his head when she took his cock into her mouth.

"Christ, you're good at this." Kaleb fucked her mouth as she took him deeper and deeper into her mouth. When she cupped his balls and gave them a small twist, he nearly came right then. But he wanted to be inside of her when he did. Lifting her up off his cock, he pulled her into his lap and took her breast again. Letting it go with a small pop, he stared into her eyes.

"I'm going to mark you again, all right?" She moaned and nodded. Lifting her breasts for him, he pulled the tip into his mouth and nipped. "We need to ride in bigger cars."

"We need to learn constraint." He smiled at her and lifted her over him. "I want you inside of me so badly all I can think of is you stretching me."

Lowering her slowly, he couldn't help but marvel at the way her face changed with each inch. Every time she rocked forward, he rolled his hips up and down for several seconds until he couldn't take it anymore. When she was settled over him, his cock buried as deep as he could go, she started rolling her hips over him, riding him with slow, strong strokes.

"I'm going to come this way." He grabbed her hips as she spoke in breathless puffs of words. "I'm not going to wait for you to come with me because if I did, you'd take too long and I want my release now."

"I'll come when you do." He cupped her ass, bringing her clit to his groin. "You're so tight around me when you start to strangle me with your climax, I've no choice but to follow you."

Her scream startled him. Kaleb felt her body milk him as she held onto him as he watched her come. Rolling her to her back, he moved in and out of her until she came three more times. He loved this about her, her ability to make him feel like the best lover in the world. And she was all his. This time he moved his mouth to her pounding pulse and snapped his teeth into her flesh.

His own release nearly took his breath away. He knew he was close, but the way his climax took him, he felt as if his entire body was involved. Even his hair seemed to ache to fill her. His balls filled again almost immediately. When he lifted his head, she looked at him, and he saw her sow there. Tilting his neck, he cried out again when she bit him deeply, taking more of him inside of her. Coming in her again, he knew that this time was different, this time they'd bonded on a level that even he didn't understand.

He held her to his body as she licked the wound closed. Realizing that he needed to do the same for her, he raised his head enough to swipe his tongue over her and was startled by the taste. Looking down at her, he frowned.

"Something is different." She nodded but said nothing. "What are you feeling right now? I mean other than like the most sated woman in the world."

Her laughter took some of the worry off him but not entirely. When she closed her eyes, he knew that she was taking inventory of herself, and he did the same. He felt different to himself as well. Checking in with his beast, he found him to be content as if he'd just had sex with her as well. That had never happened to him before.

"I feel like my bear, my sow, is not clawing at me. Like she's been laid, too." He nodded, holding his breath. "But there's something more here. Not just the sow but...like I have several people...no, not people, but several animals inside of me now and not just the one. And they're all acting like they'd fucked all night."

"Me too." Sitting up, he pulled her with him so that she was on his lap and not over him. While she pulled on her pants, he tried to think what this meant. Nothing, not a thing came to mind. "I don't know what happened to us."

"Are we in trouble?" He assured her that they were not. "Then let's go and see if Kennedy has popped that kid. I'm pretty sure no one will know what we've been up to, and I, for one, feel really good."

He didn't have the heart to tell her that everyone would know just what they'd been doing in the back seat of Jimmy's car, and not only that, he had a feeling that Samuel might know what else happened. Kaleb almost wanted to convince Thor to go home with him, but knew that just prolonging this wasn't going to change the outcome.

Getting his own pants on, he went to the trunk and gave her one of his shirts. It looked like a dress on her, but he smiled. He would have to buy her an entire store of clothes if they couldn't learn to control themselves. When she leaned against the wall of the elevator a few minutes later, he decided that buying her new clothes all the time was a small price to pay to have her whenever he wanted. Life was suddenly very rosy.

Chapter 10

Ansell hung up the phone and sat there for several minutes. He tried his best to calm his mind, but the fucking cunt was still out there. And as soon as he could, he was going to kill her and Sweeney, then flee the country. He was nearly ready to go now. The soft knock at his door had him bark for the person to enter, and he looked at his butler of fifty-some years.

"Mr. Sweeney is here, my lord. He said he wishes to speak to you." Dewitt turned his nose up before continuing. "I do believe he's been rolling in something unpleasant. He reeks of animal."

Ansell wasn't concerned with the other man's smell, but he did tell Dewitt not to let him sit on any furniture. If he stank, which Ansell had no doubt he did, there was no sense in him leaving his odor around for him to have to smell. Telling him to leave him in the main hall, Ansell picked up the house phone.

The man at the other end didn't speak when the line was connected. There was no need for communication between them. When Ansell called him, he knew what he had to do. And Sweeney was going to be his next job.

Simply putting down the phone, he stood up. The Thornton woman was next. And when she was gone, so was he. There was no point in waiting around for whoever she might have told about him to come looking. Time to move on and upward, Ansell always said about any forced moves. He'd already made his arrangements with his plane and his money.

Things had been going on here for longer than any place he'd ever been. He supposed that most of it had to do with having Sweeney nearly worship him. The man would have done anything for him, but for this one failure. And now he had to go. Ansell had learned over the years to never leave anyone behind. The house would have to go as well. Burning it to the ground with the dynamite he had placed throughout the entire foundation would ensure that no one would find one scrap of evidence that he'd ever been there.

He hated to leave, but it was a way of life for him. Ansell had already set up his next house and staff; the only one going with him was Dewitt. A movement across the lawn had him stiffen, but he realized it was his man coming to do his part in his job to rid himself of Sweeney. Ansell knew that he had one more day to find and bring her to him, but Ansell had heard about the incident at the house of Samuel Payne, and he knew as surely as he was standing there that Thornton wasn't going to come to him easily. Time to cut losses and go.

He didn't pick up the phone when it rang. After the first ring, silence filled the room. His man, a man whose name he didn't know, was in place. Now all he had to do was open the doors to the terrace and invite Sweeney in. But not quite yet.

He'd had the woman, Thornton, looked into before this. She'd been a model cop and had done things in her short life that would have impressed even him had she not been what she was. Head of the Secret Service for several years, she'd kept the president at the time from being killed twice and had been present when he'd been sworn in, as well as the next president who took his place after eight years. She'd been the lead on several homicides that had put her front and center in the paper, but she'd remained aloft during the trials, even going so far as to only come to the court house when her time to be a witness required her to. Once she'd started working for Sweeney, Ansell wondered why she wasn't the captain, as she was much more suited to the job than Sweeney ever would be on his best day. But she'd been looked over. Or so he'd thought.

A look into her records, the ones that Sweeney had gotten, stated that she'd had no desire to be anything more than a detective. Never wanted to be in the limelight, as she'd called it. Her days as front man were over, and she was content to be the one who worked hard for her checks; she didn't want the big job. He was both saddened by the potential that she could have given the smallish town and glad for the fact that he would not have lasted as long as he had. Ansell both admired and hated her.

And now he knew where she was at every moment. It had cost him a great deal, but the man who now followed her every movement answered only to him. Ansell needed only to give the word and she'd be as dead as Sweeney was going to be very soon. Sitting back at his desk, he rang for Dewitt. Within seconds, Sweeney was brought in.

"She's running amok. I can't tell you how many men she has at her beck and call." When Sweeney started to sit, Ansell raised his hand. "Something wrong?"

"Yes, you reek. What the hell have you been into? You smell like…Christ, you smell like wet dog and piss at the same time." Ansell stood up and moved to the doors and opened them. "Let's take this outside so you don't smell up my house."

He stepped out first and nodded once. It was the signal needed for his man to take whatever shot he needed to take Sweeney out. Once the cop stepped out onto the deck, he dropped to his knees almost immediately. Blood poured from his chest and forehead. When he dropped the rest of the way, falling to his face, Ansell leaned back against the railing and stared at him as he bled out. One down and one to go.

"You should have done what you were told." Ansell knew that he couldn't hear him, but he continued anyway. "Now you're going to be with the rest of the staff when the house goes up. They'll find your body, no doubt, but there won't be too much left of you when it goes."

Ansell saw the man move away, but neither of them spoke. He'd move on now, having been paid in advance. If he ever needed him again, he'd have to go through the hotline and jump through what felt like a thousand hoops to get him to come wherever he was again, but it would be well worth it. Ansell had actually contemplated having him take out Thornton, but he wanted to do her himself. He wanted to watch her as she realized he was the one who was going to kill her.

As soon as he went back into the house, he called Dewitt. Simply telling him it was finished, Ansell knew that when he looked out onto the decking again, there would be no sign that anyone ever lost their life there. And any blood stain there would be gone as well. Nothing to ever let anyone know that Lyod Sweeney ever existed. Just the way Ansell liked it. He had thought to leave him as part of the dead already there, but he'd reconsidered, deciding instead to move him away from the house. He was afraid if they found a cop there then they might dig deeper into what had happened. Ansell did not want anyone digging into his life any deeper than he allowed. He really needed to get gone and now.

Turning to his computer, he contacted the man watching Thornton. When he came online, Ansell wanted to tell him to take her now, but he wanted her to find out that Sweeney was dead first. And when she did, he was sure she'd try to run. Smiling, he thought of her trying to get away from him, and decided this was the best plan he'd had in a while. Taking out his informant as well as the cunt Thornton was nearly too much fun. But he'd love every minute of it.

"She's still at the hospital with that Payne family. I think the Payne woman is about to birth her kid." Ansell cringed when he thought of a child. There was very little that he hated more than small creatures, and infant ones made him positively ill. "She and a bevy of men are standing in the waiting room with some other chick. I can take them all if you want. No extra charge. They're a fucking bunch of rich dicks with nothing more to do with their time than fuck and spend money."

Ansell smiled. He knew that Ernie Couch hated the rich and actually found it to be entertaining at times, but right now he had him wait. "I might have you take out a couple more before this is all over...depends on how much anyone of them will miss her. But I'm thinking she might just be a piece of ass for Jonas and nothing much more."

"Whatever you say, but I'm thinking there is more to this than that. He can't seem to stop touching her. Kind of sickening. He kisses her neck, and she nearly comes all over him. The other chick, too. Some big guy has his hand on her thigh right now, and I'm just waiting for him to drop before her and suck her pussy. Might just happen yet." Ansell was surprised to know that Ernie was so close to them that he could see that much, but impressed that he'd taken it upon himself to see that he was. "There's a woman here, too, in a wheel chair. She seems to be some sort of big deal to them all. Nearly foaming at the mouth to do her every call."

"That would be Payne's mother. But don't touch her even if I tell you to take the rest. She and I have a history." Not that Ansell wanted to have to admit it, but Summer Payne had saved his life once. And for that alone, he'd spare her. At least until she did something to anger him. Then she'd be just as gone.

He'd been ten and his father was on a drunken rampage again. But when he drew back the tree branch to hit him with it, Summer had stopped him by standing over Ansell's nearly lifeless body and telling his dad to back off. By then he'd lost so much blood that Ansell knew he was dead. When he'd woken in the hospital a few days later, he'd tried to find the pretty woman. But her husband, an abusive prick like his own dad, had forbidden him to see her. It was years later that he heard that her husband had beaten her and her son more than Ansell's own father had beaten him.

"Stick with Thornton. I want her to find out that her boss is done." Ernie laughed and said he was glad it was finished. "He came here smelling like dog. Do you know why?"

"Not why he'd smell like dog, but she did rough him up a bit. Her and that man of hers. Some other man bobbed his head on the car hood a couple of times, but there weren't any animals around." Ernie laughed. "Could be he likes fucking them. His wife sure hated him for some reason."

"She was a bitch and was trying to get more than she deserved." Ernie had taken her out two days ago, when it had become apparent that Sweeney had fulfilled his usefulness. She would be a part of the house when it blew, as she was already set up in the basement to be found with a few others he'd cultivated. "Call me when there are any developments. And try to see if you can record her reaction when she finds out about Sweeney. I really wish I could see that."

Ansell closed the connection and sat back. Time was running short now, and he had a lot of things to do. Going to the kitchen to find Dewitt, he asked to speak to him. Within ten minutes, he knew the plan of leaving. Both of them would be gone within minutes of Thornton being killed. Ansell went to his room to gather what he wanted to take with him. Not too long now.

~~~

Kennedy held her little boy and clung to her husband's hand with her free hand. The little bugger had picked a fine day to be having for his birth. She looked up at Samuel when he squeezed her hand.

"I'm supposing you want to hold him." Samuel laughed. "I'll be handing him over to you but for now, I'm bonding with him. He's a mite on the tiny side, don't you think?"

"He's perfect." Kennedy grinned at the nurse who was standing close by. "You've done a good job there, Mrs. Payne. Healthy little cub to take after the two of you."

"He'll be big and strong, too." Kennedy had fallen in love with her son the moment he'd been put to her chest. And when he nursed right away, she'd felt as if the entire world could go to hell and she'd be just fine. She looked up at Samuel when he continued. "When do you want to call the others in?"

She wanted to tell him never but knew that wouldn't go over well. Her *seanmháthair* would be very upset with her if she tried that. Looking at her son again, she spoke softly to Samuel.

"We've yet to single out a name. What do we call him for the rest of his life? Boyo? How about *ár gcuid mac*?" She told him it meant *our son* when he asked. "I'm thinking we're to name him before they come in."

"I've been thinking on that as well. And I know that naming him for my father is simply out of the question, but naming him for yours is something I'd very much like to do." She looked at him and felt tears fill her eyes. "Kendal Samuel Payne is what I had in mind. We can call him Kendal or Kenny if you'd like."

"Kendal please. My father...he'd be proud of him. And of ye. Said that any man who tamed me would have his vote. Wish he'd been around to meet you. I do." Handing him his son, she watched as pride and love filled his face. This man above all others she'd known had given her the world. She wanted to give him some of it back. "There's something you should know. About the estate in my homeland. I was contacted several weeks ago about the sale of the town just over. If you're a mind to sign the contracts, I've made a purchase for us. And if you've a heart for it, I'd like to have Michael take over the running of it when he comes of age and is done with his education."

Her sister Kaitlin was wedded now as well, and she and her husband were expecting their first child. Kaitlin was now running the general store with Daniel back in Ireland, too. She missed them both so much. The two of them were as happy as could be, and were coming here once they'd birthed their own child. Kennedy told Samuel it was time to let the others meet their child.

Her *seanmháthair* was the first to hold him. Samuel handed Kendal off to her as soon as she walked into the room. While his mom looked on greedily, Kennedy realized how very lucky she'd come to be. Wiping at the tears, she looked at Summer when she handed her a tissue.

"You've done very well, my dear. Very well. You've managed to tame the savage lion, have a lovely home, as well as a manor, and now you've a son to carry on the family name. I'm very happy to call you my own." Kennedy blew her nose. "Now we'll have none of that. You'll have this old woman blubbering like an old fool if you don't stop."

"I'm so happy. Ye've made me feel like I belong." Summer nodded and held her hand. When *Seanmháthair* asked if she was all right, Kennedy nodded. "I'm just the luckiest woman in the world."

"Not as lucky as me." Samuel kissed her quickly on the mouth and pulled her to him. "I've a gift for you if you don't mind me giving it to you with all these people around."

He pulled out the pretty blue box before she could answer and opened it. There inside was the most beautiful bracelet she'd ever seen. Diamonds and emeralds fought for brilliance with the darkest rubies she'd ever seen. He pulled it out and put it on her, much to the enjoyment of all those with them. Michael patted Samuel on the back.

"Ye've a hell of a wife there, brother mine." Kennedy felt her heart swell every time Michael called him that. "But I've something, too. I've found me a wife. I'll be bringing her around when all this ado is over with."

Everyone congratulated him, and she kissed his cheek. When he wiped at the tears, she smiled at him. "Your future wife, does she know you're not much of a catch?"

"Aye, she does. Doesn't care a whit though. Says she'd settle with me until someone better comes along." He smiled at her. "You'll like her. She's a bit like you, bossy and all."

Nodding, she couldn't talk over the lump in her throat. They'd done well, the three of them, despite all that had happened to them. When the nurse came in to tell them visiting was over, Samuel asked for her *seanmháthair* to stay. It was finally time to let her know what they'd done.

She took it well considering the amount of money they'd spent to make it happen. The house for her on the property wasn't a mansion, but it was very lovely. And she'd have servants, too, to help out, along with the added bonus of being so close to her and her new family. Michael had also said he'd be honored to take over the estates. But he wanted to finish his education as well as marry his girl. The love of the right person could do that.

After everyone left, Kennedy leaned back on the bed and watched Samuel with Kendal. He was so gentle despite his size. Kendal yawned and then smiled at them both. Closing her eyes, she listened to him talk.

"You're a big guy, aren't you? I can see you taking on the bad guys with just one hand." She laughed softly. "And you'll protect your sisters and brothers, right? You being the oldest, you'll have to be the one to tell them what to do. However, so you know, if you have a sister anything like your momma, she might take you to task if you try to boss her around. Your mom is the same way."

"What a thing to say to him." She opened her eyes to glare at him. "He'll be thinking his mother is a tyrant."

"Nah, he'll love you no matter how bossy you are." Samuel got up and brought Kendal to her. He already looked more at ease with him. When she had her son in her arms, she smiled down into his small face. "Your dad would be so proud of you."

"Aye, he might. I've a mind to take you both home again." They'd not been able to travel as much in the past few months because of the baby, but now she wanted to see her green hills again. "I've decided to bring some of the things back with us this time to furnish Kendal's room. I've spoken to Hawk, and he'll take on what I give him."

Samuel crawled into bed with them and kissed her neck. "Whatever you need to do, you know I can work from anywhere." She nodded and leaned back against his chest. "I'm exhausted. You having a baby is tiring."

In minutes he was asleep, and she listened to his heart beating beneath her. When the nurse came in a few minutes later, Kennedy reluctantly gave her Kendal to take to the nursery so they could rest. When she snuggled down into Samuel's arms, she reached out to her friends and family to see if they were all right. Thor spoke back to her.

"Do you suppose all men are idiots or just a select few?" Kennedy told her most and asked her what happened. *"Kaleb seems to think that because I said yes to marry him that it should be right now. I think it can wait a few weeks, months, too, if you want to know the truth."*

"He asked you to marry him? Wow, that's wonderful. And I take it he gave you a lovely ring, too?" She told him he hadn't. *"Well then, you hold off for as long as you can. Any mon who pops the question without benefit of a ring deserves to have to wait. You tell him I said so, too."*

"Yeah, I think I can handle him." Kennedy waited, knowing there was something more. *"Something happened tonight. While we were having sex. I think we...well, I was going to say evolved, but I'm not sure that's quite right either."*

Kennedy felt a finger of fear touch her. She reached deeper into the other woman but was blocked, and for whatever reason, that made her more fearful. Both of them were silent for a while. When she spoke again, Kennedy had a feeling that Thor was as afraid of this as she had been anything else in her life.

"We were having sex, as I said, but when I bit into him, it felt as if I was coming so hard that I was going to explode. Then something changed. It was as if every part of me, even my fingernails, came, too. Then I felt something...something's enter me. As if it was just waiting for that moment to take me over." Kennedy got up from the bed and moved to the chair. The heater was there, and she turned it on. Chilled to the bone, she put her hands on it as Thor continued. *"You must think I'm a real nut-ball. Not to mention talking to you about my sex life as if we're great friends."*

"Aren't we?" For some reason, Kennedy wanted Thor to be her best friend. She'd been a part of Samuel's life when he'd been but a boy. Kennedy wanted to know that

child through her. *"I've no idea what has happened to you. What does Kaleb say? Surely he noticed, too."*

"He felt it. I'm not sure what he knows, but he's...did you know that he is two thousand years old?" She didn't, and wondered if Samuel knew. *"Yeah, this witch did this to him and now he's telling me I have the same thing. Oh, and let's not forget the fact that there are faeries running around here to protect me. My life isn't what it used to be."*

Kennedy burst out laughing and looked over at Samuel when he sat up. "I'm talking with Thor. She's having issues about her new life."

"Kaleb is talking to me, too. Something about they've changed or something. I don't understand just yet." Kennedy nodded and got up to go back to the bed. "He seems to think that whatever happened to them tonight is going to be something I'm not going to like."

"He's over two thousand years old, did you know that?" Samuel nodded as he pulled her into his arms. Thor spoke to her again before she could get completely settled.

"I have a question. No biggy if you don't know the answer, but what the hell am I supposed to do as a bear?" Kennedy laughed. *"I mean other than be all furry and shit, what possible reason would anyone want to change into this huge lumbering thing that eats honey and sticks?"*

"I'm reasonably sure you'll find something useful to do with her. And she can protect you as well. Did you know that if you're hurt as a human, or even a bear for that matter, that if you shift, you can heal yourself?" Thor asked her if there was a book on this. *"Not that I'm aware of. Kaleb should talk to you about your abilities. I take it he hasn't."*

"No. We've been dealing with other shit. Did you know that my father was in town? I meant to tell Samuel and his mom, but I got sidetracked. He'll hang around until I give him what he wants or he beats the shit out of me again. Then he'll

move on. But he's pretty much bad news, and he hates Summer." Before she could ask her why he'd hate such a lovely woman, Thor continued. "When we were kids, Summer took me in for a while. My mom was sick back then a lot, but now that I've given it some thought, I'm pretty sure she wasn't so much sick as she was beaten up. I don't know if you know this or not, but my mom killed herself one day when I was ten."

"No, I didn't know that. I'm very sorry for your loss. Me own mother is a bitch. I've dealt with her for years before I finally told her to leave me be. Michael and me sister Kaitlin are doing well now without her influence." Kennedy settled next to Samuel and smiled. "Do you think ye can come to my home tomorrow? I'd very much like to have a sit down with ye. And the baby, you've not seen him yet."

"Yeah, we were having sex in the car in the lot when you were in the throes of that stuff. I'll come over, but…well, I don't do kids. I know nothing about them and have never even changed a diaper before. Hand me a gun and I'm fine. A kid? And you might as well shoot me with the first thing 'cause the second one will put me over the edge." Kennedy was enjoying her candor and wondered if she was being so blunt because they were miles apart, but for some reason, she didn't think so. "I guess you're tired. I suppose I should go back to the bedroom and try to get some sleep, too. The cook here is eyeing me like I'm going to muss up his kitchen or something. And Ana is asleep on my leg. Maybe you can figure out what I'm to do with a faerie as my guardian before I come over."

Kennedy assured her that she would. And as soon as the connection was closed, she shut her eyes. Sleep took her almost immediately. Tomorrow she'd talk with her face-to-face and things would be well. She hoped anyway.

Chapter 11

Thor watched the news reel run again. There was something off about the whole thing, and she wanted to see if she could figure it out. When the cook — what the hell was his name? — came into the room, he set a large mug in front of her. She sniffed it and looked up at him.

"It is plain coffee, my lady. No sugar and certainly no cream. I poured it for you myself." Tomas...that was it. When he started to leave, she called him back.

"Do I make you uncomfortable?" He opened his mouth and closed it twice before he finally nodded. "Why? Are you afraid of me?"

"Not really afraid of you, but...I know very little about you, and you are very...." She waited for him to finish, but he did that pursing thing with his mouth again, like he'd done last night when she told him she just wanted to sit in the kitchen.

"My mom loved to cook. You wouldn't know that, but it's true. And when my father had just beaten the shit out of me, I'd go in there to settle myself. The room smelled like she did, you see." She motioned for him to sit down and after several seconds, he finally did. "My father wouldn't have gone into the kitchen if it was the only way out of the house and it was on fire. It was a woman's domain. Anyway, I don't cook, wouldn't know how to make toast without having someone turn the stupid toaster on to the right temperature for me. But I could eat. When there was food enough. And there my mother would be my mom. She was sort of free of him, I guess, and she loved on me as much as she could."

"She died, I understand." Thor nodded. "The kitchen is not a woman's domain. I happen to love the room myself. You just make me feel inadequate."

"Me make you feel that way? How the hell did you come up with that one?" He started that mouth thing again, and she slammed her hand on the table. "Look, we're going to be living together for a long time. And I'll not improve with age if you don't let me know what I can do to make you like me."

"You're very blunt, aren't you?" She grinned and nodded. He didn't look comfortable, and she knew that whatever he found lacking in her, she was going to try her best to fix it. For him. Because despite his prudish ways, she liked him. "There was a man here yesterday. A man who said that he was your father. I'm assuming that he is the man who made you seek refuge in my kitchen."

"He's part of it. What did he want? You didn't lend him money, did you? If you did I'll make sure you're paid back, in full." He shook his head and smiled. "You turned him down."

"I had him removed from the property." She laughed hard, and he finally joined her. "Mr. Thornton said that you had told him he was to come here for an envelope. He claimed that you said he could have the master's car to use as well. Master Kaleb does not loan out his cars."

"I'm sorry you thought I was like him." When Tomas started to protest, she lifted her hand. "It's okay. I would more than likely have thought the same thing. He's slick and he's sly. But he's not welcome here. Ever. And if he tells you differently, you're to tell me immediately, and I'll deal with him."

"He needs to be arrested. I've never seen a more...how did he have such a child as you and be the way he is?" Thor didn't know, but she was going to have to deal with her father again. "Miss, I would like to say that I am sorry. I should never have judged a book by its previous owner. You are a fine addition to the master's household."

"We're okay then?" Tomas nodded. "Good. I like you. Now I need your help. Look at this when they play it again. Tell me what you see that seems...well, it doesn't seem right."

As the feed came around again, he reached for the remote that was right beside her. When he paused the video, she moved closer to the screen and looked hard at it. Then she saw it. Turning to Tomas, she grinned.

"You found it." She looked at Kaleb when he spoke and then back at Tomas, who was staring at the screen like he was going to find what she did or know the reason why. Finally after several moments, he looked at her. Taking pity on him, she walked to the screen and pointed to where the blanket lay over what she assumed was Sweeney's body.

"What do you see here?" He told her a road. "But the road seems to be moving downward, like he's lying on a hill. But look at the blood. Where does it go?"

Tomas got up and walked to the television. He stared at it for several seconds before he looked at her, shocked.

"The blood is going in the wrong direction. Why would it do that?"

"Because whoever put him there wanted everyone to think he was killed there and not somewhere else. But logic wins out. If you kill a man on a hill, the blood would go in the direction of the landscape, not defy physics and go uphill. Whoever planted this body there poured the blood, no doubt from someone else, to hide the fact that he was murdered elsewhere. The body was planted, not killed there." Tomas looked at her, then at Kaleb.

"I shall have luncheon on the table at one, sir. It will be pot pies." When he turned to her, he winked. "I am glad we had our talk, my lady. Shall you need anything...and I do mean anything...I am your man."

Thor looked at Kaleb when Tomas left them. She was confused. But Kaleb seemed to understand. He pulled her into his arms when he was close enough to do so.

"You've won him over, I see. He only has luncheon for someone when he likes them. When Vinnie comes over, it's repast. I don't think he cares for the dragon." Thor looked up at him. "I heard you two talking. I guess we're going to have to deal with dear old Dad again."

"I'll take care of him. Maybe I can eat him or something." She sat down on the couch again and turned off the television. "I'm pretty sure we both know who planted Sweeney there. I just have to figure out where he was killed."

"I've had Stephen go to the house that you told us about. It's empty like you said it would be. I'm guessing that he had another one that no one knows about." She nodded, thinking about the lengths that Lipscomb was going to. She also wondered about his game plan.

"Sweeney said that he needed me to go to Lipscomb. Why? It's not like I know much more information about the man other than he was there when I was hurt. And last I heard that's not really enough to kill someone over. At least not really. I mean, Lipscomb is big fish, but other than a few things that I suppose about him, there is no real evidence to put him at the scene of any of them." She leaned back and closed her eyes. "I found a few things, a warehouse and a shipyard, but there was nothing there when I went to check them out."

"Did Sweeney know you were going there?" She looked at him. "They were partners, right? And you would have been a loyal and dedicated cop and told him where you were going and when, right?"

"I did. So you think that he made it so I'd find nothing?" Kaleb nodded. "I think you might be right. I mean the warehouse alone looked like he could have performed surgery there."

"We could go there now. Or we can go out into the woods behind this house and I can show you how to shift into my sow." Her body shivered at his voice. Kaleb could make her feel things no one else ever had. "Are you up for it?"

"Wait." She stood up when he did but didn't move toward the door. "What if I can't do this? I mean, what if my bear or whatever she is decides she doesn't want to come out and be a bear? And what about those other things inside me?"

"She wants out. I can feel her, and I'm sure you can as well." He ran his finger down her arm and the animal in her reacted. "Feel her? Feel her slide along your skin and change you?"

Her arm darkened with thick hair. When she looked up at him, Thor could see his as well. His bear seemed to take part of him and make it his own. She nodded once and took his hand when he offered it.

They were standing in the woods when she felt something stir along her body. It wasn't the bear this time but something else. When Kaleb said her name, she felt something take her, and fear had her screaming his name as she changed. Then suddenly she was out.

"Take deep breaths." Thor tried to pull away from Kaleb, but he held her tightly. "Not just yet. You have to learn to get your feet under you. Christ, you scared the crap out of me."

"Kaleb?" She heard herself talking in her mind but what spilled from her lips was anything but human. *"What happened?"*

"I don't fucking know." He sounded so terrified that she felt fearful herself. And when she looked down at her body, she knew real terror. "One minute you were shifting and the next you were changing into ten different things at once. But when you fell to the ground, I nearly died. Christ, what the hell was that?"

"How the hell should I know?" She tried to stand up but fell over. Her body was huge, but it wasn't a bear like she'd assumed she'd be, but a large feathered animal. When she looked up at him, she realized that he really was afraid. *"Is this what happened to us last night?"*

"I think so. And so you know, you're not alone. I did the same thing you did. I think the only reason I'm not a falcon right now is because I have a tad bit more control." She felt him stroke her back. "You're the most beautiful bird of prey I've ever seen."

"You shifted, too?" He nodded. *"I don't want to do this anymore. How do I be like you?"* She glared at him when he laughed. *"I'm going to knock you on your ass if you laugh at me again."*

"You're going to be naked when you shift back and I, for one, can't wait. And as much as I'd like to tell you you'll be okay, I find you to be very sexy right now." She huffed. "I don't mean I want your bird but you. I want to fuck right now."

Thor realized then he was naked, too. And when he told her to think of her human self, she closed her eyes and saw them all there. All the animals that had come to her sometime last night. Fear had her looking at Kaleb again as her body seemed to melt into herself. This time it was painless and made her feel like she could do this. Whatever this was.

"There's a wolf, dragon, and what appears to be a human but not." He told her it was a vampire. "I think there's a faerie and the lion, too. Do you have those as well?"

"Yes. I'm thinking that we're taking on whatever shifters we've had contact with. When did you meet Hawk? He's the only bird I know." She shrugged and closed her eyes again. When she opened them this time, she knew she was just herself. "I want you."

Moving over his lap, she settled herself down over him with his cock straining between them. Wrapping her hand around him, she rocked her body against his and moaned. When he laid back, she put her free hand on his chest and watched his cock.

The tiny pearl of cum on the tip had her wanting to taste him. When she scooted back to licked him, he growled at her. Watching his face when she leaned over him, she nearly came when he threw back his head the moment she touched him with her tongue.

Thor loved tasting him this way. He let her explore him as much as she wanted. And when he started to rock his hips up, filling her mouth with his cock, she swallowed him. The feeling of him in the back of her throat made her hum. And that nearly had him bucking her off.

"Again. Christ, do that again." She hummed again and again, and every time he begged her for more. "I'm going to come. Let me come on you." He pulled her away, and she sat up just as his first stream of cum sprayed over her. Hot and thick, she rubbed it over her body as he emptied himself over her. When he sat up, she moved back from him to stand up, and he nearly flipped her to the ground. She then turned to look at him when he pulled his hips to hers from behind.

His cock slamming into her took her breath away. And as he took her to the ground, his body bent over hers, she pressed back against him, giving as good as she got. Thor felt her own climax rising up. And when Kaleb slid his fingers into her pussy from beneath her, she screamed until her throat was raw with it.

Neither of them moved, not that she thought she could. Her knees were beginning to ache a little when he shifted his weight off and rolled to the ground, taking her with him. Looking up at the clouds, she tried to get her breathing under control.

"Did I hurt you?" She smiled at his question. "I'm sorry. I don't know what came over me. One minute I was as sated as any man could be and the next, I needed to dominate you or die. Christ, it felt as if I were some sort of animal."

"You were, but I loved it." She rolled off him and to her side. Thor rested her head on his chest and stared at him for several minutes before she spoke again. "It was the wolf. I think he needed his time with mine somehow."

"I felt them, too. This is the strangest thing that I think has ever happened to me." She could relate to that statement. "We need to talk about this and other things."

"I know. But can we wait until we get this crap with Lipscomb finished? And I'd very much like to see if I can find anyone in the department that wasn't in with him." She sat up and looked around. "I guess my clothes are toast."

"I have something in the woods you can put on. I usually leave things there when I want to run or need to run. I think you can wear my shirt." She watched him walk away from her and laughed at the fact that his entire back was covered in dirt, twigs, and rocks. When he moved to a tree and rubbed against it with his back, she realized how much of a bear he really was. Forty minutes later, after putting on something that fit, they were sitting in the kitchen with Tomas and his wife having a nice luncheon.

"My lady, I have a friend that works in the mayor's office. I can make a call to him to see where he stands. It might help you deal with what is going on if you knew you had an ally." When she told him it would be fine, he went to the phone and called. Ten minutes later, he sat down. "I do believe you'll be pleasantly surprised. The mayor is not only in your corner, but he has set up a taskforce to look for you. Someone from his office is to call you back within the hour."

Thor looked at Kaleb and smiled. "They miss me."

~~~

Ansell answered his phone without thought to why it would be ringing in the middle of the night. And when the man started speaking on the other end, Ansell had to ask him to slow down twice before he finally shut up.

"Now calmly tell me what the hell you're talking about. What do you mean the mayor is at the Jonas house? When the hell did that happen?" Ansell reached for his robe and pulled it on as he waited for an answer. "I've asked you a question and while I can understand that I said to shut the fuck up, now is not the time to be obtuse."

"He showed up about two hours ago. I never thought it was him until I realized the plates were different than that Payne guy's. When I got up close and personal with it, that's when I saw it was the mayor's. He even has a sticker on the side advertising who he is." Ansell cleared his throat once, and Ernie laughed. "Sorry. I'm calmer now. As I said, I thought it was Payne. He comes over a lot and when I moved closer to see if I could get a look-see, what do I find? He all cozied up on their couch having a drink and laughing. Right now they are still in the dining room, but from what I can tell, they'll be moving to the inner part of the house soon."

This was not good. Sweeney had it figured out that he needed to end the mayor, that he had too much sense to let this go. And when Sweeney had mentioned that Thornton had gone on this spree of killing other cops and men, the man had shut him down faster than he'd seen before. And he was untouchable, too. As many times as he'd tried to pin something on him, he came out smelling like a fucking rose every time. And now he was with the one person who could put Ansell at the scene of a crime.

"Kill her. All of them. I want them dead now." There was a pause. "There a problem, Craig?"

"Yeah, you might say that. This house has a protection around it. I know you think what I'm going to tell you is fucked up, but I swear to you the minute I step within five feet of the house, I can't move. And when I tried to shoot at the hedges just to test that out, the bullet just stopped the same distance to the house as I can walk up to it. Picked up three casings that never made it to the greenery around the house."

"You're telling me that there's magic there?" The man didn't answer. "What the fuck are you smoking? Or are you drinking on the job? If you can't do this, then perhaps I'll find someone else that can."

"Good luck with that. Like I've been saying to you, I can't get anything to the house to cause any of them harm. I'm just letting you know." Ansell wanted to throw the phone across the room but waited to hear what other nonsense Craig was spinning. "You might want to know that the police are gathering together, too. My informant at the precinct said that there's an all-call out. Meaning that every available officer has been called in. But no word on as to what the hell they're being called in for. But I would simply just blow the house if I were you. I understand you're good at that."

Ansell ignored the jab about how he left his affairs. It was none of his business anyway, but the other worried him. An all-call, the mayor at the cunt's house, and a house he couldn't get to. Things weren't just fucking up. They were right out there where he needed to get out of town or end up in jail fucked. Picking up the briefcase that had sat near his bed since yesterday, Ansell moved to the door.

"I want you to stop now. Get out of town. If they're aware of what's going down, then it's a safe bet that they know someone is out to get the bitch." He nodded to Dewitt as he went to the garage. It was way past time to get the hell out of there. "When you get settled elsewhere, I want you to give me a call. All right?"

Silence. It wasn't just the kind where you think you've been hung up on or the call dropped, but profoundly noisy in the background with no voices. When the scream tore across the receiver, Ansell wanted to hang up but was so caught up in the events that he couldn't see that he waited on the line. A shuffling noise alerted him that someone was going to speak.

"You're next." Chills raced down his spine as the man on the other end of the phone spoke. Ansell dropped his phone and pulled out his gun. Whoever was coming for him was going to have to come through his gun, and Ansell was going to shoot first. A hand on his shoulder had him turning and firing at the same time.

"Sir?" Dewitt had his suitcase in his hand as he dropped to his knees. The blood seeping down the front of his shirt had Ansell grabbing him to ease him to the ground. Dewitt coughed once, and blood poured from his mouth as he stared up at him. "I don't understand."

"I'm so sorry, my friend. I thought you were someone else. I had no idea...I'm so sorry." Ansell knew he was dead a few seconds later. Closing his eyes, Ansell sat there holding his hand until he heard the first explosion going off in the house. He barely made it to the garage before the rest of them went.

Pulling out of the now burning garage, Ansell looked in the rearview mirror as he sped away. Things had taken a turn for the worse and he was pretty sure that whoever was on the other end of his cell had not just killed Ernie, but truly was coming for him. He planned to be far away.

If, he realized, there was ever going to be someplace that was far enough away. Ansell had a feeling that he was dead no matter where he was.

Then it occurred to him. She'd done this, the fucking cunt that hadn't died when she should have. It was time to make her pay. And even if he had to get himself killed, which now that he'd thought about it was highly likely, he was going to end the bitch. Taking a turn at the next light, he was passed by several fire engines. By the time he'd made it to the Jonas house, he had a plan. Going in full tilt was the only way to make this happen.

Chapter 12

"What do you mean, you killed him?" Kaleb tried to think how to answer Thor's question without pissing her off more. It wasn't a hard question, but she seemed bent on being mad about this, and he couldn't for the life of him think why. He was glad now that the mayor had left ten minutes ago so he wouldn't see her in a snit.

"I knew he was on the property and I went out to confront him. But then I heard him tell this other person that he should blow up our home. And I'm fond of this place. You live here with me, and so does our staff." She took a step toward him, and he could see she was madder than before. "You wanted him to blow up the house?"

"I wanted to find out who else he might be working for. I wanted to question him about how he found us and who else knew. I thought it would be wonderful to see if anyone else has it in their head to blow our home." He'd never thought of that and told her so. "No shit. Damn it, Kaleb, now what? Have you called the police?"

"They won't find him." She stared at him for several seconds, and he felt the need to explain. "There won't be enough of him out there for anyone to gather up and take to the morgue. When what I consider mine is fucked with my boar takes over. He wasn't happy with him being so near his mate."

"You tore him up?" Kaleb thought about explaining to her that his boar had, not him, but he was afraid she'd hurt him. Again. When she was riled like she was now, she could be a little on the violent side. Taking a step back from her, he started to tell her what else he'd done. He put his hand on his chest where she'd hit him not five minutes ago.

"I might have warned the man he was talking to that he was next on my to-do list." She took a step toward him, and he put up his hands. "I love you."

Kaleb had meant to say that in a different way, but he'd been nervous. His plan was to give her the ring that was currently sitting on his desk and beg her to marry him. She'd said yes, but he wanted her to have the ring he'd had made for her when she said so again. But now it was all messed up.

"I have a ring this time. It's on the desk." He moved to the desk and nearly dropped the box twice before he could get it in his big hands. "I had this idea to make love to you in front of the fireplace and have you all sated and naked and then ask you again. Tell you then how much I love you and would forever."

She didn't say anything nor reach for the box when he held it out to her. Kaleb decided that he'd tell her the whole thing. But the look in her eyes had him rethinking that. Instead, he dropped down in front of her on one knee and opened the box.

"You do this now?" Kaleb was startled by the anger in her voice. "You propose to me now when I'm in a pissy mood. Is this the way you think you can get around me?

Distract me for a while and you think I'll forget that I'm pissed off. Well, it won't work."

"I never thought it would." When he saw her tighten her hands into fists, he took her hand into his and kissed it. "What I mean is, I love you with all my heart. I never thought of those things about the man out there because all I could think of was protecting you. I know that you're all bad-assed now, but there is still a part of me that says, 'she's mine and I have to make sure she's okay.' I never meant for you to be put into a position that makes your job more difficult."

"I don't like it when I don't know what's going on. It's why I never do Christmas." That shocked him. He loved the holiday and all it meant. Kaleb thought briefly of last Christmas at Samuel's house and how much fun they'd had. "If you do this again, I'm going to be really pissed at you."

"Duly noted." He kissed her hand. Then opening the box, he showed her the ring he had for her. "I told you this was what I wanted for you. Opals to match the creaminess of your skin, emeralds to go with the temper I've seen you have, and sapphires to compete with the fire in your eyes when I make love to you. Do you remember me saying that to you?"

Thor nodded, and Kaleb slid the ring onto her finger. The opal was the centerpiece. It had taken him the longest to pick out this stone from all the others. It was almost pure white with the smallest stream of gold through it. The emeralds were dark and old. He'd found them centuries ago when he'd been in another country. He'd nearly forgotten about them until he'd been trying to find the gold he'd had melted down to form the band. And the sapphires were the richest blues and silver he could find.

Their color and clarity had been, in the jeweler's opinion, the most gorgeous he'd ever seen. All Kaleb could think of was how much they reminded him of her.

"This does not get you out of trouble." He smiled and pushed the ring to her knuckle and kissed it. "You're not going to get this back if you change your mind."

"Never." He stood up and pulled her into his arms. "You really need to start believing that I'm not going to let you go. I'm in love with you and I'm yours."

"Sire, mistress." They both turned to look at Ana, who was hovering just over their shoulders. "There is a problem. Should you like to turn on the television?"

Kaleb reached for the remote and flipped it on. Before he could ask Ana what station, he found he was on the right one. The fireball was massive.

"The reporter is saying that it was a bomb. Several." Calina sat on his shoulder when he sat on the couch. "I think it was set."

"You think it was set?" Ana smacked Calina on the shoulder. "You think a bomb was set in a house in the middle of a residential area. My goodness you're brilliant. Perhaps you could be a consultant on the police force. With your ability to tell the obvious, they'd never have to leave the offices."

Kaleb had to bite his hand hard. It never seemed to stop between the two of them. Calina would say something that she more than likely thought very profound and Ana would cut her to ribbons. He nearly lost it when he looked at Thor and could see she was having a hard time not laughing as well.

"You know I never know if you're being sarcastic, said no one ever to you." Calina sniffed hard at her friend.

"You could just say something like 'Calina, that's very brilliant of you, but—'"

"I'd never say the words 'Calina' and 'brilliant' in the same sentence. Unless it was something like, 'Christ, Calina, you are amazingly, brilliantly stupid.'"

"Ladies, perhaps we could—" They cut Thor off with a flutter of their wings. It wasn't long before they were both out of the room and who knew where. He looked at Thor when she spoke. "Well, they do give us a great deal of entertainment, I guess."

He couldn't help it. Kaleb started laughing so hard that he had to stand up to breathe properly. And every time he looked at the small dusting of sparkly dust on the sofa arm, he would go into more peals of laughter. Christ, he hoped this was the setting for rest of his life. He'd live to be a million if this was what he had to look forward to.

Sitting back on the couch, they sat down to watch more of the news. It was assumed that, like Calina had pointed out, it was set. The bomb killed at least one man, and he'd been outside the house when the explosion occurred. Nancy, the onsite reporter, said that it looked to her as if he might have been shot, but the police were looking into that.

"I'm betting it's not Lipscomb." Kaleb had to agree with her. They simply were not that lucky. "And I'd bet anything that the man outside the house wasn't supposed to be there. He more than likely was leaving, too. Did you notice the luggage?"

Kaleb hadn't but was impressed that she had. "It could have been Lipscomb's. He might have been in the blast, too, and blown away, leaving behind his underwear."

She laughed as he'd hoped she would. When her head leaned against his shoulder Kaleb closed his eyes. This was a part of his life that he'd never thought to have. And now he had it all.

"When I was a young boy, I'd been mean. Well, not really mean but a little more on the side of going that way than not. My mother despaired of me ever living past my tenth year. She thought me of what now is called a hoodlum. And the day I met the witch, I had made her cry." It still bothered him even after all these years to think what he'd done to her. The tears had hurt him more than any switch his father could have taken to his hide. "She'd made this sweet bread for my brother's birthday and I'd knocked it off the table in a rage. I'd never been so sorry about something in my life, not then or since. She never said anything to me but sat down and cried. When I went to comfort her, she'd asked me politely to go outside and play. I ran to the woods to hurt something."

"You found a witch instead." He nodded. "My mother cried a good deal when she was alive. But it was hard for me after a while to feel much for them. She never tried to leave him, not once in all those years. I asked her once if she loved him, and she told me not ever. Why would she…? I guess I'll never know now. What did the witch to do you? Did you upset her, too?"

"No. I was angry. So mad at something that I wanted to destroy anything I could get my hands on. It wasn't until years later that I realized the only person I was mad at was myself. And by then it was too late. But I'd heard her crying, too. I'd thought it was my mother, but when I found her, I nearly left her where she lay." Kaleb closed his eyes on the painful memory. It was, too. His heart still bled for what he'd done to the one person who had loved him above all others. But he'd thought to make amends with someone else.

~~~

"You'll not hurt me, young boy, or I'll harm you in ways that you'll feel for decades." He'd come out from behind the tree he'd been hiding behind and looked at her. "You go on back to your house and get your father. He'll know what I'm about."

"He's dead." He wasn't, but Kaleb and his family had been telling people that for so long that he didn't think of him in any other way but dead. He'd left them years and years ago. "I can help you. I'm the man of the house now."

She'd laughed at him, and he had started forward to show her a thing or two about him being manly, but he stopped when he saw the blood. There was so much of it he wondered if there was something else with her.

"I've been helping her, but I don't think it's doing me a bit of good. And I can't leave her either." Kaleb nodded and stepped toward her, taking off his shirt. When she took it from him, he bent down to help her put it over the body of the child he'd just noticed. "You cannot be touching me without me telling you it's okay. Do you understand me?"

Kaleb had nodded and told her he wanted to help her. "I won't hurt you. I swear to you. Let me help you and take you to my mom. She can sew anything up. Last week she made me new clothing."

"I bet she did. But it's not sewing I be needing. It's only help and a few things from the earth. Do you think you can do that for me? Get me the ingredients that I ask for?" Kaleb nodded and stood up. That's when he'd seen that the body was that of a little girl. "She's none of your concern. You just look at me."

He was sure she was dead, but when the little girl looked up at him, he felt something move over him. The witch said something to him, but he didn't hear her. It was the child, all torn up, that had his full attention. When the witch snapped her fingers at him, he looked at her.

"She approves." Kaleb had no idea what that meant back then, and there were days when he still didn't. The child had been mauled by a wolf and she was going to die if he didn't hurry with his task. It took him nearly an hour of running around the forest to get just what she needed from him.

By the time he made it back to them, the girl had her eyes closed again. The witch, who hadn't been hurt at all, was standing over a small fire and putting the things he'd already brought to her in a pottery bowl. He handed her the last three items and stepped back.

"You still wanting to help me?" She hadn't looked at him when she spoke, but Kaleb nodded all the same. "It's powerful magic that I'm using. Something that will save her if it's not too late."

"I said I'd help you, and I will." She looked up at him and seemed to look deep into him. Kaleb remembered thinking that she was looking at his soul, but at the time knew that was impossible. But now he knew that she'd done just that.

"I need your promise and your blood." The promise part was harder for him than anything. Blood he could do, he thought, but he'd never kept a single promise in his life. "You'll do it still."

"I will." And he knew deep in his soul that he would, too, even at the risk of his own death. "I'll keep your promise and give you my blood. All of it if you need it."

He'd been sincere, too. Kaleb had no idea what she wanted from him in a promise, nor how much blood she needed. But when he glanced at the child again, he knew that she would be worth it.

"Give me your wrist then." He put it out there and noticed how dirty he was. Taking it back, he wiped it on his equally dirty clothing before offering it to her again. "You're sure?"

Kaleb nodded and felt the blade he hadn't seen until that moment cut into him. Wincing at the pain, he watched as his blood dripped into the bowl and sizzled with the other ingredients. When she told him to step back, he looked at the wound and saw the small scar.

The words she spoke he had never heard before. She made the flame higher at one point, catching the bowl and its contents to flame. When she sat back and looked up at him, he smiled when she did.

"You're very powerful, did you know that?" He knew that he was simply a boy but nodded, thanking her for saying so. When the brew was cooled, Kaleb realized how dark the evening sky had gotten. But he couldn't leave them just yet.

The witch had given the mixture to the little girl. It wasn't working at first, so Kaleb leaned down to her and whispered in her ear. He told her that she had to be all right and that she needed to keep her mommy happy. He even told her that he'd hurt his own mother and regretted it more than he did anything else in the world. When she swallowed the first drink, he smiled at the witch and sat back while the child drank the rest.

"You did a great thing for us." He shook his head at the witch and stood up to go home. "I'll never forget this.

Ever. But you can never tell anyone what you've done here today, except the one who will hold your heart."

"Nobody will want my heart. I'm a mean boy and can't control my temper." She nodded at him and touched his arm when she returned his shirt. The power that surged through him made him stagger. "You gave me something."

"I did. Go, before your mother overly worries, and enjoy sweet bread with your family." He didn't tell her that there'd be no sweets. That his mother had saved for weeks to make the one he'd ruined. But he went home to tell his mother he was sorry, sorrier than he'd ever been. Picking flowers on the way to soften what he'd done, Kaleb walked into the kitchen just as his mother was putting dinner on the table.

~~~

"We had a cake that night and once a week thereafter. For some reason, the ingredients would show up in the pantry and my mother wouldn't question it. The blood on my shirt either." He looked down at Thor when she shifted in his arms. "Do you know what she gave me?"

"Yes, I think. She gave you life." He shook his head. "Then what? If you tell me that she gave you her daughter, I'm going to strangle you."

"No, she didn't give me the child. And for the record, I never saw either of them until many years later. But she gave me the ability to be the man she said she knew I'd become. It wasn't until I turned twenty-five that she came back and gave me the immortality. By then my mother had passed on, and my brother was...well, Langley was already turning out to be worse than I'd been when younger. He...he turned out to be ten times the ass when he realized he could live forever."

"I understand, probably more than most would. Some people, like your brother and my dad, think that everything should be handed to them on a platter all done up with gold and silver. And now this guy is doing things that could be considered worse but really, it's all the same. A person wanting more than he deserves and will kill to get it." She nodded and then looked at the television. "I guess we should either expect company from this or figure out where Lipscomb has gone into hiding at."

Kaleb couldn't wait for this thing to be over. But he stood up to help her make some calls and do some Internet research.

~~~

Ansell found the house easily enough. He'd never been there, but the address that popped up when he'd done a search on Jonas's name led him right there. But getting in might be an issue. There was more security surrounding this place than he'd ever seen. And most of it was in the form of high electrical fences.

Ansell made four calls before he was able to find someone to come out and assist him in getting in the gates. Two of the men had told him that they were on jobs; the third guy had told him to fuck off. If he wasn't sure this was going to be his last big job, Ansell would have hunted the man down and killed him himself. But things were going to end here today, and there was no going back. By the time his man showed up, Ansell was on edge.

"You certainly took your own sweet time." Ernie Couch simply smiled and got out of his car. They'd met at the diner in town and were now making their way to the house again. "I thought you'd be here an hour ago."

"Nope." That's all he said, and Ansell felt his temper raising a little more. When he stopped walking, Couch stopped, too, and turned to look at him.

"That's all you have to say?" Couch shrugged and turned to walk on. "I'm not finished talking to you. I want to know why you took so long to get here when I specifically told you an hour ago."

"It took me longer, that's all you need to know." He hadn't even turned when he spoke. Ansell caught up with him and put his hand on his shoulder to jerk him around. He was going to shoot this prick and try to find someone else. But he hadn't expected his gun to go flying and one to be pointed at his head so quickly.

"Now. This here is what you're going to do. I'm going to lower my gun and you're going to back the fuck off or I'll kill you, take your money, and leave you here to fucking rot. Do I make myself perfectly clear?" Ansell nodded. "Good boy."

When the gun came down, Ansell had a second to think he could simply take the man, but he was sure he'd be just as dead as Couch had threatened. When Couch said nothing for several seconds, he turned and started walking again. Ansell was sure that one word from him would make him leave. Ansell decided that when this was finished, the man was dead.

"I need to get inside the gates and to the house." Couch nodded but only looked over the fence. "I don't know what to expect with the household when I get there."

"Big." That was ever so helpful and Ansell nearly told him so. But Couch continued before he got himself killed. "And I'd say that this isn't the only problem you're going to run into. I'm betting the house is ten kinds of locked up."

"You mean you can't get in." Couch shrugged, and Ansell felt his temper snap. "Stop doing that. Either answer me properly or don't, but shrugging is beneath both of us."

"Okay. The gates are locked down with interlocking electrical fencing, which means that whoever put this in did so in a way that when one section is cut, the overlapping wiring will take over, keeping the power running. The high tension wiring at the tip is barbed wire, ten strains of it. It's viciously spaced so that even if you tried to go over it, you'd be cut up so badly when you got to the other side, you'd bleed to death. Around the perimeter, you see those nice, deep cuts in the walls? Those aren't foot holes for an idiot to use for climbing; those are traps." Couch picked up a thick stick and rammed it into one of the sections. The outer walls snapped shut, and he could see spikes holding onto the log. After a few seconds, it released it. And when it dropped, Couch showed it to him. "I'd say that those bite marks are five or six inches deep, would you?"

Ansell nodded. Christ, no wonder Ernie hadn't try to breach this thing. "What do we do now?"

"Nothing. We try to get in and we're dead or wish we were. We wait for one of them to come out." Ansell started to point out that someone had come out and killed his predecessor, but he didn't. The man was on his own about this part. "Unless, of course, you have a better idea."

"No, I don't." They moved back to the diner and got their cars. Parking them closer to the gates than Ansell thought smart, Couch leaned down into his seat and closed his eyes. The man was actually going to take a nap? Now?

Ansell sat next to him, thinking about all the things he'd like to do to the sleeping man but knew in the end, if he was going to get the cunt, this man was his only hope. Leaning back in the seat, he closed his eyes as well. He was leaving getting into the compound to this man. He was certainly paying him enough to do so, but he was so going to kill him afterwards.

Chapter 13

Samuel walked up beside the car with the sleeping men inside and looked at Stephen. Neither of them said a word as they walked by them. They'd been on patrol in another area of the grounds when Thor told them about the car. She said she'd seen it when she'd been out in the woods.

"Do you suppose we should kill them both?" Stephen looked back at the car when Samuel asked him. "I mean, they can't be here for anything but bad news."

"The man under the steering wheel is Hawk. I think he might be pissy with me if you tried to kill him. Besides, I'm pretty sure he can take you." Samuel turned back to look at the car and saw the driver wave at him before settling back in the seat.

"Why is he helping out this asshole?" Stephen laughed. "You hired him. Damn it, Stephen, what if I hadn't had you with me? I could have killed him."

"You could have tried. Hawk is a little more than a simple shifter. He's...he has a great deal of me in him." That made no sense, and he asked him what he'd meant. "We've traded blood enough where he can bite if he wants, and has been known to feed when he needs to heal quickly. I would imagine that he is either going to make a tasty meal of Lipscomb, or he's planning to serve him up on a platter for Thor."

Either sounded like something Stephen would do. In the few weeks she'd been there, all his friends had told him how much they liked Thor. Samuel hadn't realized how much he'd missed her either until now. He walked to the gate and punched in the numbers.

"Do you suppose she'll let us in?" The gates opened slowly and they both moved through the gate before it was completely open. Samuel knew that Stephen could have simply gotten in without the aid of the gates, but he couldn't. As soon as this shit was over, Samuel was going to talk to Kaleb about getting the same security firm to come to his house now.

"How's the baby?" The question startled him out of his thinking, and he looked at Stephen when he laughed. "Long nights or somewhere else?"

"Both. And he's fine. Kendal is growing more and more every day. Gab is over at the house now with Kennedy. I think they're planning something for Thor to welcome her to the pride." It was that or they were planning to help them get Lipscomb. He was never sure what went on in their minds when they got together. "I think you should find your mate and have a few on your own."

"No thanks. I think I've missed that boat anyway. It's been entirely too long and I'm much too set in my ways to take on someone who will want to change me." Stephen and he rounded the corner to the house and stopped to stare. "Christ, did you know about this?"

"No. I'm not sure...do you suppose they have to have maps to get around?" Even the landscaping looked like it was huge. "I don't think I want Kennedy to see this. She might want one for herself."

The house looked like an old mansion. There were long white columns that stretched from the wide wrap around porch to the third level of the house. Large, wide windows graced the front of the house, and all eight of them looked like they contained fifty panels of glass each. The door, a solid affair, was a double door that he was sure a car could be driven through. Along the front porch were rocking chairs, ten or more, each of which had a nice little table sitting by it. And at each end of the front part of the porch was a swing, complete with pillows.

"You think he has a decorator?" Samuel slapped at Stephen when he asked. "I mean look at this place. Holy hell, this is nice."

Kaleb met them at the front door. Thor was standing behind him, and she didn't look all that happy. When they shut the door behind them, he looked at Kaleb.

"She's mad because I told her to stand back while I made sure it was you." He looked back at her as he continued. "I think she thinks to protect me from the bad guys."

"I will be the bad guy if you don't let me be myself." Thor came around Kaleb to stand in front of him. "I want to come and stay with you for a few days. He's going to be dead if I don't get out of here."

"I don't think that's such a good idea. Lipscomb is right out front, and he's gunning for you." She huffed at him, then left them standing there. Stephen started to follow her when he stopped suddenly.

"Faerie? You have faeries here?" Kaleb nodded and pointed to the molding around the room. Samuel looked up and didn't see anything at first, but then one of them moved and he saw them.

"Christ." There must have been a thousand of them. One of them came down closer and stared at Stephen. When she bowed before him and fluttered away to sit on Kaleb's shoulder, Samuel had to ask.

"Something I should know?" Stephen looked to be in pain, and when he turned to look at him, Samuel could see that his beast was coming forth. "What's going on?"

"Faerie blood. It's...amazing." Stephen backed up and bumped into the wall. "I have to get out of here."

Samuel nodded and reached for his friend. Before he could touch him, one of the faeries flew in front of him and slapped Stephen in the face.

"Buck up. Do you want to cause a scene in this house?" She flew around him twice more before she was in front of him again. "Do you want to be cured in this house, or do you want to insult my mistress?"

"I want to drink from you in your other form." The faerie laughed, and Stephen reached for her. Suddenly, Thor was there with a knife to his throat.

"Touch her and I will cut your heart out and feed it to them." Stephen looked at Samuel and then at Kaleb as Thor continued. "Ana asked you a question. Die or be able to come in this house all the time?"

"You've no idea what you're asking of me." Thor nodded at Stephen. "I want to be able to come here, but if there are faeries, I'm fucked."

"Calm your beast." Samuel watched the faerie Ana as she moved closer. "I cannot work with you if you're snarling like an animal. Calm him."

Stephen snarled at her but looked at Thor. "You're hurting me. Will you please remove the knife from my chest?"

"When you can behave. And know this, friend of my mate's or not, I will kill you if you harm anyone in this house. I'm not as big and strong as you, but I think I might have the advantage right now." Samuel saw Stephen wince. "So if it's all the same to you, I'll hold you this way. Answer. The. Faerie."

"Yes." The hissed answer had spittle coming from his mouth. Ana moved closer to Stephen, but she didn't touch him until Thor nodded, then let him go.

Stephen stood there for several seconds. And the longer he stood staring at Thor, the calmer he seemed to get. When he pushed from the wall, Samuel started forward, but Kaleb's hand on his arm stopped him.

"You could have been hurt." Thor shrugged at Stephen. "What would you have done if I had not calmed? Surely you wouldn't have killed me."

She put the knife in her boot and stood up. When she crossed her arms over her chest, Samuel thought of every time she'd done that when they were children. He smiled because he knew just what she was going to say.

"Well, it's a good thing we don't have to find out the answer to that, now isn't it?"

Stephen stared at her for several heartbeats before he threw back his head and laughed. Ana landing on his arm had him tensing up.

"You'll have to teach me that trick of yours." Ana shook her head at Stephen. "And what if I come to another home where there are faeries? What will happen to me then if I should harm them?"

"You'll die. But that will not happen, my lord. In any house that is a part of the pride, you will be safe. I shall not allow you to be killed with such a horrible death as the mistress had in mind for you." Stephen looked at Thor, then back at Ana when she continued. "She has a mind for this, I think. To protect what she can and kill what she deems...unworthy. Are you, my lord? Are you unworthy of the mistress?"

"I hope not." Ana moved up to stare into his face and then floated to the ceiling again. All at once every winged creature there moved down to greet them. Thor looked at him.

"You okay?" He nodded. "You're not going to go shit crazy on me, are you? I mean, I can put you down if you want."

"Fuck you."

Samuel went into the main room just off the entrance hall and stopped in his tracks. There were no words to describe this room. He looked at Kaleb before speaking again. "Holy cheese and crackers, man. Why the hell have you been hiding this place? This is amazing."

"Well, I've had a lot of time to collect." Kaleb went into the room that Samuel decided would pale beside most museums. Samuel wondered briefly what else he'd had time to do.

~~~

Hawk moved in through the gates as soon as they opened. He just hoped this harebrained idea worked. Why they were letting the bad guy in was beyond him, but Stephen said it would be taken care of. Of course it would. Hawk just knew that he was going to be killed as soon as he stepped in front of the house.

"He certainly knows how to live." Hawk didn't say anything to Lipscomb. First of all, what the hell was he supposed to say? And secondly, it was hard to hold this voice for that long. Shifting to another person was hard enough; talking like them was murder. Moving toward the garage, he found what he'd been told to look for. Some of this plan was ingenious.

The guns were hanging on the wall just like he'd been told. There were five of them, all newer and covered in dust. Hawk had a moment to wonder how the hell they'd pulled that off when he looked at Lipscomb. These guns, he'd been told, held only blanks, as did the guns on both their persons.

Lipscomb was staring at the cars as if he were going to fuck one of them. When he ran his hand over the polished dark red surface, Hawk wanted to tear his throat out.

"Do you suppose when she's dead they'd miss one of these babies?" Hawk didn't bother answering. The Lotus was gorgeous, but he had one similar to it in his own garage. Some things a man just didn't touch. The first thing was their mates. The second thing was their babies. And cars were all their babies.

"I think if you don't fucking get your ass in gear, I'm leaving you." Hawk tossed the gun at him and nearly laughed when he fumbled it. They moved out of the garage and into the yard just as Kaleb was coming out. So far so good. When he pointed the gun at the man and fired, Kaleb went down.

"The girl is mine." Lipscomb didn't bat an eye when he moved toward the house. "I'm killing that bitch if it's the last thing I do." Hawk watched him, knowing that it was going to be the last thing he did.

The door hung open and Lipscomb moved up the steps like he owned the place. He didn't even hesitate when he fired the weapon Hawk had given him at the butler. Then when Samuel was suddenly there, he shot him as well. Things were going just as they'd planned. But when the younger woman came out and stood in front of them, Lipscomb seemed to freeze.

"You've been very busy, I see." She looked at him and then back at Lipscomb as she continued. "I'm going to enjoy taking you to jail. If you make it that far."

"Jail? In the event you didn't notice, I have the upper hand here." Hawk glanced at Lipscomb and noticed he had a gun pointed right at the woman. Hawk hadn't met her really, but he thought this was Thor. He'd bumped into her once about five years ago and knew that she was something special. He'd not known what until just then.

"You with him?" The question startled him, but Hawk shook his head. It was past time for him to own up to his part of the plan. Besides, he wanted to shift again. The guy he'd turned into was shorter than him and was a tub of lard.

"He's here to kill you. Seems to think that you've shit in his oatmeal or something." Hawk laughed when she nodded. "I heard you were something. I just wonder how long it will take before this fucking idiot understands just how something you are."

"You fucking bastard." Winking at Lipscomb, Hawk shifted to his true form. "What the fuck? What…how the hell did you do that?"

"Magic, you moron. We all have it." Lipscomb took a step back as Samuel stood up and continued. This was epic, Hawk thought, and decided to watch until bullets started flying. A few more minutes of this and he'd have to mark this up as one of his favorite days.

"You're dead. I killed you." Lipscomb looked over at Kaleb when he sat up, too. "There is no way in hell you were able to survive that."

"Well, it seems you're very wrong about that." Kaleb stood up and jerked the gun from Lipscomb and cracked it open. "Blanks. We knew you were coming. Fuck, you're stupid, aren't you? I'd think a man like you would check that shit first. Or at the very least, have your own weapon. Didn't they tell you in bad guy school that you never take a gun from someone else, and you never ever piss off a woman? Your batting average has taken a major dump today."

The gun came from seemingly nowhere. And when he fired it at Thor, everyone seemed to freeze for several seconds. Then...Hawk blinked several times to make sure he was seeing what he really thought he was seeing. Mother fuck. Taking a step back, he waited to see what happened with this shit.

Thousands of faeries were swarming from the house. Most of them stopped at Thor, but when she sat up, those who didn't moved to Lipscomb so quickly it was as if they'd known what they were going to do even before the bullet left the gun. And when they landed on Lipscomb, the screams were enough to make him want to close off his ears.

They tore him apart. Not in large pieces like his arms and legs were torn off, but in small pieces that Hawk knew no one would ever find enough even for DNA purposes unless they looked really hard. And he doubted anyone would care that much. The speed in which they did it made him still not believe it. In a matter of seconds,

Lipscomb was gone, simply gone, and the only thing left to even show he'd been there were his bloody clothes and the gun. Everything else about the man was no more.

"Thor?" Hawk moved to the porch, giving the clothing on the ground a wide berth. He got to where Kaleb and the other faeries were and smiled when Thor started cursing.

"I'm fucking fine." Kaleb pulled her into his arms as she tried to stand up. "I'm really fine. I told you this might happen, and would you listen? Oh no, you said he'd never pull the trigger. He's the one that hires men to do that sort of thing. I told you—"

"Shut up." Hawk moved off the deck when Kaleb told his mate to shut up and went to stand by Samuel, who was still staring at the clothing.

"You do know that he's not there, don't you?" Samuel looked at him with a blank stare. "Lipscomb, he's dead you know?"

"I didn't know they could do that." Hawk nodded. He did. In fact, he'd seen it done once before. Not the actual killing but the aftermath of one. This one was clean in comparison. "They seem so…so tiny."

"Yeah, but they're a massive front when they band together like that." Hawk put out his hand. "I'm Russel Hawkmen. Everyone calls me Hawk. I spoke to your wife a few weeks ago."

"Yes, the furniture guy." Samuel nodded as he continued, and Hawk turned so neither of them could see what was left of Lipscomb. "I guess you're going to go to Ireland with her soon and see what you can fix."

"I can fix anything. The issue is whether or not you can afford me." Samuel laughed and nodded. Hawk immediately liked the werelion. "You the master of this group? You do know that they belong in a lunatic asylum, right?"

"I am. And you're right, they do. I still don't know how it happened, but I have been running it for about a year now. You're a shifter. Vinnie said you prefer to be a hawk. Is it because of your name or a general preference?" Hawk nodded without answering. It was a long story and one he wasn't thrilled to be telling to a stranger. "I see."

"Doubtful, but that's okay, too." Samuel took his hand. "Is there a place I can stay around here while we get the house squared away?"

And that seemed to be that. When they had finalized the plan for him to stay with him in the big house, Hawk told him he had a car that he wanted to store, too. Samuel told him there was plenty of room in the garage and to bring it over. By the time they turned back around, Thor was spouting orders about clean up, and Kaleb was leaning against the house. Some things never changed.

"You look the same." Hawk nodded at Kaleb. "You are still as fuck ugly as you've always been. Might be worse if you really want to know."

"Yeah, you don't look much better. I hear you've got yourself attached." They both looked at Thor. "She's not what I expected for you in a mate."

"Me neither. Great, huh?" She turned to look at them as if she knew that they were talking about her. Christ, she was more beautiful every time he looked at her. "Are you still looking for yourself a mate?"

"No." He moved away from his friend. Hawk wasn't really in the mood to talk about mates and such. And didn't know if he'd ever be. There were some things that were better off just not talked about.

Hawk moved to the edge of the woods and shifted. He'd been able to take on any animal since he was small. And it wasn't until he was in his teens that he realized that few could shift like he did. Most shifters — well, all he knew — had to lose the clothes and then wonder how to get any when they got to where they were going. Flying high over the trees, he let the wind current take him. He could shift naked or fully clothed and when he landed, his clothes simply appeared when he turned back. It was a good selling point to being a shifter, he thought.

This was his preferred method of living. Not as a human, though it paid the bills, but as a hawk. Soaring above the trees and looking down on what the world had become. When he got to his car he'd parked in a garage, he got inside and pulled out his cell. Smiling, he listened to the message from his mother.

"I suppose I should be grateful that you bothered to use your own voice on this ridiculous contraption. Just so you know, I'm not pleased with you. Who sends their mother five dozen roses for no other reason than to tell her he loves her? You should be sending them to a lovely girl. One that will give me grandchildren." Either she ended the call or she ran out of time. Either way, he decided to send her another five dozen in the morning. When he started the car up, he reached for Vinnie.

"*You said she was pretty; you lied.*" Vinnie laughed. "*I thought she'd be a lot less like Kaleb, too. I don't know why, but I thought of someone he could boss around, and she'd be all mushy about being with him.*"

"*She's a hell cat is what she is. And I would doubt that she's ever been mushy about anything or anyone.*" Vinnie laughed again as he continued. "*I don't suppose you contacted me to tell me that you're hanging around for a while, did you? It certainly would be nice to see you for more than ten minutes this time."*

"I'm staying with Samuel. He and his wife have generously offered me a place to stash my car, too. You think they're okay with what I do with inanimate objects?" Hawk rubbed his hand around the steering wheel. *"This one's got something in her that I can't part with."*

"They'll get it. And you'll be surprised when you pull your baby in how much you and Samuel have in common. He's a collector, too, but I don't think he's aware of it yet." Few knew the attachment that Hawk had with his things that didn't breath. And the fact that he could help them was amazing, too. *"He has a Porsche that could use your help I think, too."*

He decided that he'd have a look at the other man's car but wouldn't fix it. As he drove down the road, he thought about what he'd just said to himself and laughed. He knew that he'd fix the car. If for no other reason than the fact that it would call to him. And he'd never been able to turn one down yet.

"You go to sleep?" Hawk laughed at Vinnie and told him he hadn't but had been thinking. *"I was hoping that you and I could talk about a few things when you get here. The main thing is that I need a partner."*

"I don't do humans well. You know that. In fact, I try my best not to do them at all. They're a smelly, overbearing lot and for the most part make me nuts." Vinnie laughed. *"I'm serious."*

"I know, you really are nuts. But I promise you, what I need from you isn't so much a partner as a person who can come in and do the finish work. The wood work stuff." Hawk pulled into the drive at Samuels's but didn't breech the gate. *"I need you to tell me what the wood wants."*

He wanted to do it, and he was pretty sure Vinnie knew it. But there were things to consider. Things like him living here full time. *"Let me think about it. I'll tell you when I get back from Ireland with Kennedy."*

Maybe by then, after the several months he was going to be away, Vinnie would have forgotten about it and he'd be off the hook in making the decision. Hawk was pretty sure he'd not forget, and he'd be pledging to the big lion, too. He pulled up to the house and looked at the garage. Okay, this might not be so bad after all.

Chapter 14

"Mistress, there is that man at the front door." Thor looked up at their new butler, Phillip Cox. Tomas had had to quit because his mother had been ill. They hoped he'd return, but it didn't look like he'd be able to. "He said that he wishes to speak to you about a loan. I do believe he said he was your father."

"Tell him to fuck off." Phillip took a step back, and if the look in his face was any indication, they'd be looking for more help next week. This guy was too stiff anyway. "I'll talk to him. Let the idiot in."

With a nod, he left them. When he was gone, she looked over at Kaleb while he laughed. "I do believe you shocked him a little. What do you suppose the chances are he'll stay to supper?"

"I don't care. If he took the rod out of his ass, he might be okay, but he gives me the creeps. Can't we please try and see if Butler and Brigitte will come here?" Kaleb laughed harder. "I want to be able to say what I want when I want to without anyone looking at me like I'm sub-human."

"I doubt very much he thinks you're sub-human. He more likely thinks you're something of an oddity. Or maybe something that should be working in a locker room." She snorted. "See? That doesn't help either. Maybe if you tried to be more...I guess less manly around him he'd change his mind. But I love you just the way you are."

"Thanks, I think. And I like me, too, so he'll have to fuck off as well." They both looked up at the door when Phillip cleared his throat. "Don't tell me he decided not to come up."

"No, mistress. It's another person. This gentleman says he's your brother, sir. A Mr. Langley Jonas." Kaleb growled, and she laughed at him. "Shall I allow him to come up as well?"

"Two birds and all that. Yeah, show the second idiot in. Set them in the front room. And don't leave them. They'll have the room stripped down to the bare plaster before you can tell us they're here." She watched Phillip leave and wondered if he'd simply go and get his things and leave now. Thor was still laughing when she and Kaleb stood to go to the front room.

"After they leave, I'm taking you upstairs and ravishing you." She shivered when he nipped at her neck. "If we make it upstairs. Right now, I'd like nothing better than to shove you against this wall and take you hard. After I eat you."

"How am I supposed to deal with my father and your brother if you're making me wet?" He growled at her to do it quickly. "You too. I might have a thing or two I'd like to do to your body."

The door was open when they entered, and Phillip moved out of the room, shutting it quietly behind him. Thor sat down on the chair nearest the fireplace, and Kaleb stood nearby. They both looked at their family.

Neither of them was worth the time and effort to talk to them. Especially her father. He was nothing to her long before today, and it was doubtful that anything he said now was going to change her mind.

"You gonna speak to me or you gonna have a staring contest? I don't want to be here any more than you want me here." Her father stood up to pace. "Got me into some real trouble and you're going to have to fix it. I know you have the means to do so. So don't give me any of your hard-hearted shit and hand over the money."

"No." He turned to stare at her when she spoke. "You got yourself into this, now get yourself out. I've got more important things to do than to —"

When he came toward her, she stood up. He drew back his fist to no doubt hit her, but she was much quicker. She had him in a head lock before he could make good on his physical threat. As she'd told him before, she wasn't ten.

"You're a piece of shit. Did you know that?" He struggled more and she tightened her grip on his throat. "If you make me kill you, I'll simply bury you in the backyard. It's doubtful that anyone would even care."

"You should have more respect for me than this. As much as I hate to admit it, you're my blood and you have to help me out of this. It's your duty." Her father finally stopped struggling and held still. "You gonna let me go or what?"

"Or what. I have no duties to you other than to keep you away from me. What the fuck did you do? Not that I really care. I'm still not bailing you out." Thor let him go and took a step back as she continued. "Whatever you think you are to me is gone. As of the moment you took your first slug at me as a kid. I'm over you."

"You guys are more fucked up than we are." She glanced at Langley, who she'd only just met tonight. "I mean, what the fuck girl? Give him what he wants. It's not like you're not going to live forever."

Her dad looked at Langley, then at her. "What the hell is he talking about? Nobody lives forever."

"I will." Langley laughed. "So will my brother. And if I don't miss my bet, so will your daughter. And in all those lifetimes of living, they'll be able to amass such a fortune that you'll never be able to suck them dry. Isn't that right, Kaleb?"

"Shut up, Langley. You and I are going to talk later. Right now, we're dealing with Mr. Thornton." Langley stood up and walked to her as Kaleb stood. "You touch her and I'll tear you apart."

"You mean like she'd be able to do if you let her? You have her on a tight leash, don't you? Keeping her in line like you try to do to me?" Langley sniffed her. "Hum, you smell like the two of you had been having some fun before we got here. Have you been fucking your pretty little mate here and we interrupted you?"

"Langley, I swear to Christ, I'm going to kill you." Kaleb took a step toward his brother as he continued. "I'm done with you, too. As of right now. You want something, then go out and earn it. Otherwise, never come here again."

"Oh, we both know you'll give me what I want. Or else I'll go on another rampage and kill some more little kids. You remember what happened the last time, don't you? I got into that school and tore those kids to pieces. And then what happened? Oh yeah, you gave me what I wanted in the first place. I won't go so cheaply this time." Langley sat down next to her on the couch. "Maybe this time I'll take me a little piece of your mate. You let me fuck her and I'll see what I can do about—"

Thor put her hand around Langley's throat and held him there. With her free hand, she put her gun into his groin. If she'd had a camera, she might have liked to have a picture of this. He looked like a man who had never had anyone fight back before and wasn't really sure what to do about it. When her father sat down in the chair across from them, she only looked at him long enough to see that he wasn't armed. Otherwise, Langley had her full attention.

"You want to fuck me?" He nodded once. "That's too bad. And it's not going to be possible for you after I'm finished with you. Have you ever heard of neutering someone? That's my plan for you if you don't shut the fuck up and pay attention to your brother."

"You wouldn't dare." Her father laughed and Langley looked at him using just his eyes. "What the fuck are you laughing about? As soon as I'm finished with her, I'm going to fuck you up, too. I don't take kindly to being the butt of anyone's jokes. Especially to a lesser female like she is."

"You're not very smart, are you, boy? I gotta tell you, I've pissed her off a few times over the years, but I done never had her put a gun to my dick before." Her dad looked at Kaleb, who was watching her but saying nothing. "You gonna let her treat your guests like this? It ain't very sociable if you ask me."

"I didn't ask and more than likely wouldn't anyway." Kaleb smiled at her. "Kill him."

Langley looked at his brother and she cut into his throat a little, using a little of her bear to do it. Not enough to let him bleed to death, mores the pity. But he stared at his brother with such shock and hatred that she wondered if he was serious.

"Do you really think that's a good idea? I mean, Phillip is already looking like he's going to quit us. You think having him have to clean up blood is going to make it so anyone works for us?" Kaleb shrugged and that's when she realized he was indeed serious. "Then, what do I do with him?"

"Bury him in the backyard. Like your father, it's doubtful that anyone would miss him. And no matter how many times we pay them off, they're still going to keep coming with their hand out. Your dad won't be a problem but for a few years longer. He'll either be killed by somebody he owes money to or something like that. But Langley will never give up. He's lost all respect for those who would try to love him, and has killed more people in his lifetime than I've met." Thor looked at her father and didn't feel a thing toward him other than abhorrence. She looked at Kaleb when he continued. "Just do it, love. We'll be better off in the long run if you do."

"You're not going to kill me." Her dad stood up and started pacing. "I got rights, and one of them is not to be murdered in my own daughter's house. You pay me off and I'll never come back."

"How do you kill Langley?" She was thinking that her father was going to blow up at any moment and when he did, Kaleb might kill him regardless. "If you live forever, how does one kill an immortal?"

"I take it back." She looked at Langley when he started to struggle again. The things spewing from his mouth made her realize that he really did have no respect for anyone. His threats were clear and to the point. He was going to kill her as soon as he killed his brother. And he wasn't going to have any remorse about it either.

"I want you two to just leave us alone." Thor looked at her father, who had stopped pacing and was pissed now. "Get the fuck off that there man and you let us go. I think about a grand each will keep us going. That way we'll never come back here again. Right, kid?"

Langley moved so quickly that she was knocked to the floor. The power with which he came up off the couch took her breath away. And when he shifted, she scrambled back to avoid getting hurt. Christ, he was huge and he was one pissed off bear.

His claws raked out toward her, but she was either too far away or his aim was off. Just as she reached for her bear to fight back, a movement out of the corner of her eye had her still. Kaleb had shifted, too, but he didn't waste time on being a bear. His large, sleek panther took her breath away.

"*Get out of here.*" She nodded and started to stand up, but Langley took another swipe at her. "*Honey, get out before you get hurt. I'm going to take care of this piece of shit now. I love you.*"

"*I love you, too, but I won't leave you to get yourself hurt either.*" Kaleb growled at his brother when he moved toward him. That's when she noticed her father.

He was dead. She could see that even from where she stood. His head lay at an odd angle and his body was bloodied. Something welled up, but it was gone almost immediately. It wasn't sorrow like she'd thought, but relief. He was dead. Her father would no longer be a problem to them or to anyone else in the world.

The room seemed to grow tight, and she looked up when someone touched her arm. Phillip was looking at her with such terror that she thought the man was going to have a heart attack. Before she could tell him to get out, he lifted her up and jerked her along behind him. They were in the hall when the first loud scream sounded.

"I have to go back in there. He'll kill him." Phillip stood in front of the door, and she started to knock him away. She stopped when she saw him shift ever so slightly. "What are you? You're not human at all, are you?"

Phillip let all of him go. And when he did, he bowed before her. When Ana came to stand beside him, she bowed as well before looking at their butler. She smiled when she came to light on her shoulder.

"This is his other form. He is the Lord of the Wood. Lord Phillip came to ask if he could work for you until such time that he was satisfied that you'd cause no harm to any of us. I think you impressed him." Phillip shifted back and stood as ramrod stiff as before.

"I have deemed this house one of safety. I shall allow the others to come here to work for you." Thor started to tell him that she would decide who would work for her and he'd just have to live with it when she heard another crash in the other room. "He will take back what should never have been given in the first place. And when he does, his lordship will know peace again."

"You knew what he was?" Phillip nodded at her. "And you knew what Langley was when he came here. What did you expect him to do? Give him what he wanted and put him out?"

"I did. He has done so many times before. His lordship has loved his brother for many years, but has only recently known that his love was not returned." Phillip looked at the closed door when another scream was heard. "I do believe this will be good for him as well. His lordship has needed to have closure for many years."

"To kill his own brother?" Again Phillip nodded. "So you've been watching him for a long time. Did you...I don't know, did you know about me, too?"

"No. You were a pleasant surprise to us. Not at first mind you, but you have proven that you're not like your sire." She snorted. "I have insulted you?"

"Not really. I'm not at all like my father. Or at least I hope I'm not." She looked at the door when she realized how quiet it was. "Is he dead?"

"He is...he is not as he was before. And no, my lady, you are nothing like the man who lays yonder." When the door opened, Phillip stood back but said nothing as Kaleb staggered out. Phillip helped him to the kitchen, where he sat him down and handed him a bottle of beer.

"I'm guessing you're with the witch?" Phillip shook his head at Kaleb's question. "Then what the hell are you doing here? I know you're not human, and that would have been nice to know earlier."

"It was not my place to tell you. And I am not human, no. And the mistress of witchcraft did not send me, but her daughter did." Phillip handed Kaleb an envelope as he continued. "She has been watching over you since the two of you met. There was a time when she despaired of you making it, but behold, you have proven over and over that you are a man of worth."

"The witch's daughter." Phillip nodded to her. "And your relationship with her is something more than her being your mistress."

"It is. You are very smart. When the man named Horne calls you, we would like for you to say yes to his question. And I am her mate, as I assume you have guessed." It took Thor's mind a few seconds to catch up. And when the phone rang, she looked at him. "You will tell him yes, my lady. It will be better for us all if you do."

When she took the phone from him, she looked at Kaleb. He and Phillip were talking about something. Mayor Horne asked her if she was all right.

"I'm fine. Some...we're moving things around a little bit here. New home and all. What can I do for you, sir?" She wanted to follow the men out of the room to see what was going on, but the house phone prevented her from doing that. Who the hell had a corded phone anymore anyway?

"I was wondering if you could come in and talk to me. I have a job I'd like to offer you, and the sooner we get it taken care of the better. I need a man on the job I can depend on." She started to tell him she wasn't a man, but he continued before she could. "I want you to be the chief of police here. It would be something I believe you'd be good at."

"Chief? What the hell happened to Anton? I thought he was there until someone had to carry him out in a body bag." When there was silence at the other end, she closed her eyes. "He died, didn't he?"

"Yesterday morning. He didn't die with his boots on, so to speak, but he did go sitting at his kitchen table before coming in. I had no idea the man was so old. He would have been seventy-one on his next birthday." Thor sat down on the chair, too shocked to try and stand any longer.

"I can't do that job. I'm not cut out to be in charge." Mayor Horne laughed. "Well, I'm not. I'm more of a rebel-against-the-man sort of employee. Who would I have to bitch about if I'm the one in charge? You have to be able to think of someone else for the job."

"No, you're the first pick, as well as the second and third." He laughed again. "I would really like for you to think about it. The hours are long, the pay sucks, and we'll be calling you all hours of the day and night. But the perks are, you'll get to work with me for the next two years."

They worked out a time for her to come in, and she told him she'd have to talk it over with Kaleb. There were things he might know that would prevent her from doing the job. Being a bear that could shift into anything else might be just one of them. When he and Phillip came back into the room, Ana was sitting on Kaleb's shoulder.

"We've taken care of the mess." She started to ask about her father's body but didn't when he shook his head. "I'm sorry, love. I know that you wanted to bury him in the backyard, but this way is much better. No one will ever come back on us about their deaths."

"Langley is dead." He nodded, though she hadn't asked him a question. "And now what? Do we go on as if they've never been born?"

"I would say that is the best way to do this." Phillip sat a tall glass of amber liquid in front of her. "You will need to drink more, my lady. There are things afoot that you'll need your strength for. And the mayor, he will need you in the most fit shape you can be."

"I didn't tell him I'd take the job." He grinned at her, and she had a feeling that she and Phillip were going to butt heads a great deal if he'd remained as their butler for much longer. He was too stubborn. "And I'm not sure I will."

She told Kaleb about the job offer and asked him what he thought about her being a bear and going to work with assholes. He laughed at her, and she thought if she could work with him being an ass, she could more than likely handle about anyone. Kaleb was driving her nuts.

"You'll be fine. And Phillip is right. You being on the force could be very helpful to us as weres. Not to mention you'll get to kick some major ass when the mood suits you." Kaleb pulled her into his lap from her own chair as he nuzzled her neck. "I want you."

Nodding, she started to stand up when the phone rang again. Thor wanted to ask why they had one that didn't allow movement when Phillip picked it up off the cradle and handed it to Kaleb. It was kind of creepy when he nodded at her and handed her another glass of the brown stuff.

"It's a protein shake. It will keep you and your animals happy." She started to shove it away. "It will also help you deal with them better."

She got up off of Kaleb's lap so she could speak to Phillip while Kaleb spoke to whoever he was talking to. "What do you mean, deal with them better? I think I have a handle on them."

"You cannot control them as well as you'd like. I have seen you struggle with the animals when you're tired or upset." She nodded and played with the glass. "It is only honey and tea with some fruit in it. I have not put anything in it that would harm either of you. Mr. Vicente drinks it, too."

"I don't know what I am." She looked up at him when he didn't say anything. "I've brought this on to both of us. I'm not sure what we are and what we're supposed to be."

"You're supposed to be Kaleb and Tania Jonas. You should be welcomed wherever you go simply because of that, but it will be more because of the money you have.

Lastly, and I believe you know this, you're a select shifter." Phillip sat down across from her when they moved to the dining room. "A select shifter means that you can take on the appearance of a shifter, yet you are so much more. Not like Mr. Hawk, but you can do things that other shifters cannot."

Before she could ask him what Hawk was, Kaleb came into the room. He did not look to be very happy. She glanced at Phillip when he left the room. Kaleb sat down and stared at the table for a long while before he spoke.

"Long ago there was an investment I made. I made a great many of them over the years. Some would make money, some didn't. I had plenty of time to recoup whatever I lost, and —"

"Just fucking get to it." He looked up at her and smiled. "I'm the type of person who wants the information and then details later. That way I can work through them easier. Spit it out, Jonas."

"Our investment paid off. We just recouped nearly ninety billion dollars on a product that I own by selling it to a larger company." Thor sat there for several seconds, then got up and punched him in the nose.

Chapter 15

"Your increased pay will begin from the moment you started on this case. It will reflect any and all hospital stays as well as any vehicles that you needed to rent or ammo that you purchased. There is no need for you to give us receipts. I trust you." The mayor looked at him, and Kaleb smiled. The guy was good, he'd have to give him that. But he still hadn't sold Thor yet.

"I want to be a stay-at-home wife. I might even decide to open my own firm." Horne looked at him again as if he could help him. "I have things I want to do for me."

"You'd have time for that. Whatever you want. We need you, Thor. The last administration…well, you know what they were about. The place is in need of a firm hand." Horne looked down at his desk then up at her. "I could offer you more money."

"Money is not the issue." And it wasn't. Of course, it had taken Kaleb nearly all night to convince her of that, but she got it now. When she shifted on her seat and glared at him, he remembered how much fun he'd had in teaching her that lesson.

She'd ended up in the kitchen after she'd bloodied his nose. He wasn't upset about it, but it had hurt. When he picked her up by slinging her over his shoulder, he knew two things at once. He should have checked her for weapons, and he forgot she'd had a good deal more training than he had. Kaleb was suddenly looking up at her from the floor and she was over his body, holding him there with a knife to his throat.

"I don't enjoy being tossed around like a sack of potatoes." Kaleb nodded and slowly moved his hands down to her hips until he could wrap his hands around her. "Behave. I'm pissed at you."

"For making us rich?" She nodded, then shook her head. "Or was it the way I delivered the information? Christ, do you have any idea how much I want you right now?"

He moved her down to his groin and rocked his hard cock up into her. Her moan was all the encouragement he needed. Rolling her to her back, he settled between her legs.

"Why did you hit me?" Kaleb pulled her shirt up and then her bra. Taking her nipple into his mouth, he nibbled on the tip until she was writhing beneath him. He looked at her when she hadn't answered. "Thor, why did you hit me?"

"You pissed me off. Please don't stop. I want to come." He took the nipple into his mouth again and toyed with it with his tongue while watching her face. This time when he lifted his head, she curled her fingers in his hair and pulled him back.

"How did I piss you off? I only did what you asked me to do." She growled, and he felt his cock thicken. "You like to give the order but when you don't like the results, you get pissy. Why is that? Or does it have to do with our money?"

"Your money. That was yours long before you met me." Kaleb rolled over and swatted her ass. "Ouch, that fucking hurt. What the hell? Are you trying to get me out of the mood?"

"I need only to touch you and you're hot for me. And the money that I had before I met you now belongs to us both. All of it now and any we make in the future." She didn't answer him and he slapped her ass again. "Say it, Thor. Say that it's our money."

"I'm not stupid, you know." Kaleb was slightly confused by her hurt tone. "You're going to say I have to report all spending to you and keep an accounting of it. I won't have anyone tell me how I spend my money, so you can keep yours and I'll make my own way."

"Who did this to you?" She flushed and started to move off him. "No, you'll tell me the name of the bastard who put you on a budget and monitored your...Christ, you father did that?"

"He never had any money. But I did it to myself." She flushed again, a deeper red than he'd ever seen. "I know it sounds stupid, but I didn't have anything growing up, so I put myself on a budget, a very strict one that kept me with money in the bank in the event that I needed it. I sometimes would go without food if something came up that I hadn't expected."

"Like giving money to your father." Thor nodded. "Did you ever buy things for yourself? Something that you didn't need, just wanted?"

"No. I didn't want to put myself in a position where money was an issue." She had, but he didn't say anything. "I had to make sure that no matter what happened, I could still pay my bills without depending on someone else."

"Money is no longer an issue." She shook her head, and he smacked her ass again. He thought maybe he was enjoying this a little too much when a tear rolled down her cheek. "Honey, I'm so sorry."

"I don't know if you're going to keep me." His heart took a hard twist when she laid her head on his chest and sobbed. Kaleb had never had a woman he loved so much, who could even kick his ass, be so insecure of herself before. Not sure what to say to her, he held her until she stopped crying.

"I love you." Thor didn't say anything, so he continued. "I love you with all my life. I would die for you, I would kill for you."

"I'm not all that special." He chuckled and her head came up. "What's so funny about that?"

"You're very special. I mean, look at you. Here you are lying right over top of me and you've got me hard as a rock. Yet I'm too worried about hurting you when I know for a fact that you have a gun in your pants, a knife in the top of your boot, as well as any number of things over your body that you could use to hurt me." He pulled her down for a quick kiss. "And you should also know that as of the moment you moved in here, I've had the house and all my accounts put into your name as well. Tania Jonas, I mean. So you'll have to marry me soon."

"I'm not sure how to be rich and idle." Thor moved down his body, kissing any area that she exposed with her nimble fingers. "I guess I could learn how. Do you suppose people with a shit ton of money have sex wherever they want?"

"If they don't, then they don't deserve to be rich." Thor sat up and moved her fingers over his pants, and in seconds had his jeans opened. "Thor, if you touch me right now, you'd better be prepared to have sex right here. I'm not going to move once you — "

Kaleb looked at the person touching his arm. He was ready to snarl at them when he realized he had no idea where he was right now or who the person in front of him was. When someone said his name, he looked to his right. Thor was grinning at him. She'd been trying to bring him around.

"Where did you go?" She smiled at him as if she already knew. "The mayor is asking you a question."

"You're going to pay for this." She laughed at him through their connection, and he looked at Horne. "I'm sorry. I was thinking about a few deals that I left unattended this morning. What is it you said?"

"Thor said that you're going to help her run her investigative firm. I was wondering if you could talk her into helping us out when we need her." Kaleb didn't even look in her direction, afraid she'd make him laugh. "She's a hell of a detective, and we need more like her on our force."

"I don't think we'll have a problem helping you out, but our own customers must come first." He had no idea if they would ever have any customers or what they'd do with them once they did, but Horne seemed satisfied.

After a few more minutes, they were standing in the elevator. Thor was leaning against the wall across from him and he could see that something was bothering her. Before he could ask, someone came into the cell with them. He reached for her mentally.

"What happened while I was thinking of you naked with my cock in your mouth?" She looked at him and he wasn't sure she was going to answer, but when she did, all he could

think about was shoving the person out at the next stop and taking her to the floor.

"I was thinking about how I could get you naked and your cock in my mouth. And how quickly I could make you come." When the doors opened, he grabbed her hand and nearly ran out of the building. Her laughter made him smile, but when they got to the limo, he shoved her in the back seat and told Phillip to simply drive until he told him otherwise. The faerie was laughing when he got back into the driver's side.

She was pulling off her shirt when he got in beside her. He pulled his tie off and tossed it to the floor while she stripped off her skirt. Christ, he was never going to make it. When she lay there in her thigh-high stockings, bra, and panties, he told her to stop.

"My turn."

~~~

Thor watched him move to her and felt her body respond to it. She'd been so wet in the mayor's office that she was sure that she was going to ruin his seat. For some reason the thoughts of Kaleb leaning her over the desk and taking her hard from behind would not go away. And when she'd noticed that he had that dazed look on his face, Thor knew his thoughts were the same.

Kaleb licked her ankle and she nearly came up off the seat. When he nipped at her calf, she moaned and wanted to close her eyes against the overwhelming emotions that flooded her. But watching him move up her body to where she wanted him most was too much fun. He closed his mouth over her thigh. She cried out when he bit her. Not from pain but from the small orgasm that hit her.

"You're so wet I can almost taste you going down the back of my throat." She moaned again as he continued.

"I'm going to drink my fill before I fuck you hard. Then if you're a really good girl, I'll turn you over and fuck you like an animal."

"Please." She wanted it all and he seemed to know it. His fingers slid under the elastic of her panties and her breath caught when he teased her. As soon as his finger entered her, she started riding him up and down.

"You like this, don't you?" All she could manage was a hissed approval. "I love the way you ride me. The way you scream when you come."

His mouth replaced his finger and she cried out his name. The way he ate at her made stars dance behind her closed eyes. Curling her fingers into his hair, she opened her legs wider for him and let him have her.

Kaleb lifted her up by her ass and looked down at her as he devoured her. With only her shoulders touching the seat, she could reach him. Wrapping her hand around his cock, she moaned when she felt the stream of precum fill her hand. Moving up and down his shaft, she knew that as soon as she came, he was going to join her. But she wanted his cock inside of her when he did.

"Fuck me." He growled at her but never stopped fucking her with his tongue. "Kaleb, fuck me. I want to feel your cock inside of me when we come."

He didn't so much as move her as he jerked her to him and slammed her down over his cock. Riding him fast, she picked up a rhythm that had her grinding her clit against his body every time she moved. Kaleb grabbed her hips and pulled her tighter and tighter against him with each stroke. She nearly screamed when he nuzzled her throat and bit down. Her climax ripped from her on another scream until her vision was pinpoints of light. As soon as he rolled her to her back and started to pound into her, she ran her nails down his back and felt the slick heat of his blood.

"*Come.*" He lifted his head and looked at her with blood on his mouth. "Come for me. Come now."

Her body came apart several times as she did what he commanded of her. Shattering again when he sucked hard at her throat, she nearly passed out when she bit him. As soon as his blood filled her mouth, she came again, this time losing the battle with consciousness. Everything blacked out the moment she sealed the wounds.

When she woke, she was in bed. Kaleb was sitting in the window seat that looked over the backyard. As soon as she sat up, he turned to look at her. Smiling, she motioned for him to come to her.

"If I do, then we'll never leave this room. And, frankly, you've scared me enough for one day. I thought I broke you." She looked out the window and saw that it was dark. He laughed when she asked him what time it was. "Nearly midnight. You've been out for nearly fourteen hours. I was so afraid that I called Samuel. And so you know, he's not welcome here anymore."

Laughing, she got up, just noticing that she was wearing one of Kaleb's shirts. "What on earth did he do?"

"He said I had killed you and proceeded to tell me the way I was going to be punished. It might have worked had he not burst out laughing when I asked him if I could take your body with me. Bastard." Thor could see Samuel doing that. "He thinks he's so fucking funny. I was sitting here thinking of ways to get back at him. I think I might have the perfect plan."

"I'm sure you set him straight." Kaleb laughed and nodded. "What did you do to him? Something that is going to piss Kennedy off. She can be very protective of her mate when she needs to be."

Thor sat on the window seat beside him. Kaleb pulled her to him and sat her onto his lap with a short "behave yourself." She settled in and watched the deer she thought he'd been looking at as they romped in the yard below them.

"Kennedy was madder at him than me. She said he should be horsewhipped. Then she said something in Irish and I was lost. But I'm pretty sure Samuel knew. He apologized to me and left when she did. I think they might have killed each other."

"Doubtful. Kennedy would kick his ass."

They sat there for several minutes, and she was nearly asleep again when he spoke. "I think we should really open this investigative firm. Mostly we could work for paranormals, but I think we could help out the locals if you want." She looked at him over her shoulder to see if he was serious. "We could do it, I think."

"I do as well." She looked out the window. "What would we call ourselves? Shifter Extraordinary? Shifters Finding Shifters?"

"I was thinking something more boring. How about Jonas Investigations?" She laughed with him. "Unless you want to call it Jonas' Dicks?"

"No, I think Jonas Investigations is great. I guess I'll have to marry you soon if I want to be a part of the name."

Kaleb picked her up and put her on the bed. She was going to make this work with him if it was the last thing she did. Loving Kaleb Jonas was going to be so much fun. And working with him even better. As he spooned up behind her in the bed, she wrapped her arm over his that was at her waist.

"I love you, Kaleb." He nipped her ear and told her he loved her as well. Thor smiled as she drifted off. It was never going to be dull with him, that was for sure.

About the Author

Kathi Barton, author of the bestselling series Force of Nature, lives in Nashport, Ohio with her husband Paul. In addition to writing full time Kathi likes to spend time with her eight grandkids, three children and three children-in-laws. She writes to relax and have fun.

Her muse, a cross between Jimmy Stewart and Hugh Jackman brings them to life for her readers in a way that has them coming back time and again for more. Her favorite genre is paranormal romance with a great deal of spice. You can visit Kathi on line and drop her an email if you'd like. She loves hearing from her fans. aaronskiss@gmail.com.

Follow Kathi on her blog:
http://kathisbartonauthor.blogspot.com/

www.ingramcontent.com/pod-product-compliance
Lightning Source LLC
Chambersburg PA
CBHW032123170626
46808CB00006B/2089